# THE WHISPERING

Unexpected Magic #4

---

## SAMANTHA JACOBEY

Lavish Publishing LLC

THE WHISPERING. Copyright 2021 ©

Unexpected Magic #4

First Edition

All Rights Reserved

Published in the United States by Lavish Publishing, LLC, Midland, Texas

Paperback edition

ISBN: 978-1-64900-025-5

Cover Design by: Victor R. Sosa

Cover Images: Canstock

www.LavishPublishing.com

# Contents

# Prologue

"THANKS FOR STICKING up for me, Sis," Hubert huffed. Marching to the glass exit of Spellbound, he pushed angrily against the weight of the portal. Outside, he paused as the blinds lowered, closing behind him. "Assholes," he muttered, then stomped across the parking lot to his late model sedan.

Climbing in, he slammed the door. "Aahhg!" he screamed into the empty space, his fists striking the wheel a few times before he covered his face, sobbing into the pads of flesh.

Inside the building, his only sibling was—at that moment—probably revealing her deepest, darkest secrets to a group of strangers. His chest heaved, the thought almost more than he could bear. He had known for over two years that she wasn't related to him by blood, but the appearance of her brother and sister out of the blue still took him by surprise, leaving him little time to prepare for her sudden departure from his life.

"She isn't gone, yet," he consoled himself, swiping at his stained cheeks. Starting the engine, he put the car in gear and spun the tires as he exited onto the street. Gripping the wheel with white knuckles, he recalled his visit to the prison a short time back. "Bastard."

Morcant had specified that strangers were coming. He had also tasked Bert with seeing to it that they acquired their target. "He should have said!" he fumed. "He didn't tell me that it was *her* they were coming for." Fresh tears dotted his face.

It had been pure chance that Hubert became part of Morcant Korrigan's circle of followers. A delivery to the shop on a quiet day. An innocent discussion of magic and alternate worlds, and Bert had been hooked. Groomed, even; drawn in, little by little. Easy stuff, no harm no foul. "And now Jos is part of his schemes."

Pulling up in front of his parents' house, he inhaled deeply. Calming his frazzled spirit, he closed his eyes and lay his head back against the rest behind it. "It's going to be fine."

Opening the door, he exited the vehicle, pausing again to enjoy the cool air against his exposed skin. With brisk steps, he mounted the porch and knocked loudly on the door before using his key and poking his head inside. "Mom? Dad? You guys still up?"

"It's only eight-thirty, we aren't that old," his father teased, closing the lid on his laptop to sit up in his recliner.

"Huey," his mother sang, joining them from the kitchen. Pulling him down into a firm embrace, she added, "What a pleasant surprise!"

"Not so pleasant," Hubert clipped at the dreaded nickname. "And I have asked you how many times?"

"I'm sorry, Bert dear." Angela smoothed his collar and button-down shirt. "You look handsome. Do you have a date?"

"No, I have questions." His eyes flicked to the image on the wall behind her. "Where did you get her from?"

"Get who from?" Mark asked, rising from his favorite chair and following his son's gaze

"Cut the crap, Dad. I know you guys faked this somehow." Indicating the photo, Hubert grunted, "Her real sister and brother showed up at the shop today looking for her. I want to know where she came from and how you ended up with her."

Glaring at his wife, Mark looked as if he might play dumb, but Angela slowly shook her head. "It's time, sweetheart." She patted her mate on the arm, then indicated the kitchen. "Let's make some coffee, and I'll try to explain."

"Fuck coffee!" Hubert shouted, thrusting his hands to his hips. "I want some damn answers!"

"Hey, watch your mouth, young man!" his father hollered back. "Show some respect to your mother or get the hell out."

His face flushed, Bert nodded. "Yes, sir." Holding the rigid posture, he sighed. "I wasn't that surprised. I've known for a couple of years that something was up. It just shocked the hell out of me today when they came into the Broken Match out of the blue."

"Where is Joseline now?" his mother asked, nudging him towards the swinging door that hid the next room.

"She's at M & J's. They claim that they're witches," he informed them bluntly.

"Well shit," Mark cursed. Shoving open the portal, he stomped over to the pot and began the process of making fresh brew.

"You better let me do that," his wife offered, "before you break something."

"She swore no one would ever know," he bit back. Turning to his son, he demanded, "How did you find out?"

"A DNA test," Hubert explained in the shortest fashion possible. "Why did you hide it? You had to know someone would find out, no matter what the agency promised you."

"She didn't come from an agency," Angela explained gently. "Madam Matilda Demore helped arrange the adoption."

"That crazy lady who tells fortunes? Who the hell adopts a baby from a gypsy, Mother?"

"I didn't go to her asking, if that's what you mean." His mother sniffed, switching on the pot and turning to the cabinet for mugs. "I used to visit her once in a while. I was looking for answers, and she helped me cope."

"Cope with what?" Hubert sneered. "I never knew you were acquainted with the craft."

"Don't be so dramatic," his father implored while taking a seat at their kitchen table. "We were having a hard time back then. We had been married a few years. Things were generally going well for us."

"Not everything, though," Angela added, taking a seat next to him. "We wanted a baby but weren't having any luck conceiving. And the doctors couldn't help."

"So, you turned to witchcraft," Bert accused.

"Not at all." She laughed at his simplification of such a complicated issue. "I visited Madam Demore a few times for readings. Matilda doesn't perform voodoo or cast spells. She simply guides the lost. Those who want answers they can't get anywhere else. Astrologers. Tarot readers. Millions of people trust their guidance," she defended.

"And they deliver babies, apparently," her son grunted. Choosing a mug, he poured his cup, then took the chair opposite them. "So why didn't you just tell Jos and me that she was adopted."

"That was our decision," Mark replied with a shrug. "I wasn't really for taking her in at the time, but your mother wanted a baby so desperately. When Matilda told us she knew of a child who needed a stable home, it was a big deci-

4

sion. But Joseline quickly grew on me. Once she was settled, and we realized that she was ours to keep, we decided we would never reveal that she had been adopted. We thought it would be better that way, especially after you were conceived."

"It was such a surprise, after all those years of trying." Angela grinned, leaning back in her chair with a wistful expression. "We didn't want Jos to feel less than. We loved her the same, no matter what came after."

"Well, what's coming now may test that theory. Didn't you at least ask where she came from?" Hubert took a noisy sip, his raw nerves calmed by their openness.

"We decided it was better if we didn't know too much about that," Mark confirmed. "Matilda said she had a dark history. One that might cloud her future if she were discovered. Secrecy was paramount, and we were willing to do our part."

"But how could you think she would never find out?" his son gasped, opening a disbelieving palm towards him. "One little DNA test, and it was all over but the crying."

"Well, how were we supposed to know of such things?" Angela snapped. "She's been part of our lives over thirty years. Who would have guessed people would one day have their backgrounds so deeply scrutinized. Why was Joseline having a DNA test done in the first place?"

Her face had grown red as she spoke, and Hubert swallowed, bothered by her disturbed appearance. "It was a surprise," he whispered. "We were going to put together a family tree for you guys."

Mark blinked at him, stunned at how easily their façade had been shattered. "I'm sorry, son. We should have told you. I'll call Joseline tomorrow and straighten all of this out."

"You can call, but I doubt she'll talk to you. She just found out the two of you have lied to her for her entire life. It may be a long time before she cares what either of you have to say." Standing, Hubert didn't wait for their reply as he pushed through the swinging door and exited the way he had come in only a short time before.

## ONE

## All in the Timing

PULLING out of the prison parking lot, Blake's heart beat heavily within his chest. His mission had been a success, but he felt anything but good about it. Stopping at a red light, his mind drifted back, recalling key events of the last few months and slowly turning them in his mind.

He fondly considered the day Merideth Monroe and Rider Bradshaw had shown up at his shop. A crooked grin twisted his lips as he recalled how he enjoyed sparring with the other man. "Just like his old man." The smile faded. "Before he stabbed me in the back." His brother's words leapt to the front of his thoughts. "Damn him."

Blake had helped the couple locate their secret sibling, and things had unraveled from there. "At least we saved Ezamay," he mused, pressing on the gas when the light changed. "And they're all part of my coven. Or at least they will be once they have settled their affairs and can return."

He nestled back into his seat more comfortably, the idea of growing his supporters giving him strength, and his thoughts turned to Joseline. "She will definitely make a fine addition, once we get her out from under Morcant's influence." He considered the cursed necklace they needed to remove for a moment, then became sidetracked by images of her brother. Laughing to himself, he jeered, "Hubert Tipton." The man wasn't a witch as far as Blake could tell, but he certainly carried the scent of the craft on him. "Probably from being around Josee all this time."

Either way, the girls didn't like having him around and had run him off the first night she had joined them at Spellbound. Bert would still be helping with the Broken Match, which he and Joseline owned together, but Blake doubted he would ever be of much use to them otherwise.

His thoughts back on his visit to the prison, he sighed. An idea had come to him the week before. The group had narrowly escaped, or more precisely postponed, Morcant's plans for them, and it occurred to him that having a guard inside the prison watch his brother and report back on him could prove extremely useful.

He scouted the prison for a few days, watching the shifts change as guards went into the building, and a short time later those getting off came out. Deciding on a few contenders from each shift, he set about finding out what he could about them. He quickly realized that corruption ran rampant within the system. It was highly likely his brother already owned most, if not all, of the likely candidates.

Unwilling to give up, Blake decided he needed a closer look, but the only way to do that would be an actual visit to the prison. Of course, he couldn't show up simply to interview the staff, and that meant at least a short sit down with his older sibling.

Planning exactly what he wanted to say, he would go in, make his threats, and then leave. He didn't really care about speaking to Morcant and hoped going through processing would give him what he needed, but by the time he reached the visitation cell, he felt defeated.

The guard who had taken him through and shown him to the large room had appeared friendly. Emboldened, Blake noted the nametag and had dared to ask, "So Jason, do you guys ever do favors for the prisoners?" He grinned at the guard's raised eyebrows. "Or their families?"

"Pfft," the dark-haired man had grunted. "Your brother is well connected, if that's what you mean."

Blake's heart sank, wiping the smile away. "I figured as much. Thanks anyways."

Their encounter brief, Morcant had delivered more disturbing news. If it were true and Sarah *was* expecting, things would only become more complicated. Selecting a space in front of a local drugstore, Blake shoved the gearstick into park and shut off the engine. Continuing the memory, he contemplated the dankness of the prison's visitation chamber.

The pandemic still limiting interaction, he had been alone in the room for several minutes before his brother arrived—long enough to grow a few doubts about what he was doing there. Jason had stood by the door while they waited and made no effort at further conversation. His shoulders broad, he stood stiffly with his hands folded in front of him and clasped across his belly. Defined muscles lay beneath the light blue button-down shirt; he definitely spent time in the gym.

When two more guards arrived, Morcant in tow, no pleasantries were exchanged with Jason. These two, however, were obvious friends as their banter flowed easily while they performed their duties.

As soon as Morcant took his seat, Blake felt ill. He punched up his bravado and said what he came to say, but his brother had twisted it against him, and the threat tossed after him as he left had made him regret the whole idea.

"It doesn't sound like your brother likes you very much," Jason observed, taking his time as he led Blake away from the visitor center.

"No, he doesn't." Blake ran his fingers through his dark waves, deep in thought. So deep, he almost missed it. "When I asked earlier, I wasn't wanting any favors for him."

"Yeah, I gathered that." Jason grinned at him. "What did you have in mind?"

"I just need someone who can watch him," Blake dared in a quiet tone, his eyes keeping watch around them. "I'll make it well worth your while if you pass along any news."

Jason nodded at him, the end of the hallway looming before them. "We could discuss my rate. How about a beer tonight?"

"Absolutely."

They had agreed on a location and would meet later at a local bar. Returning to his car with his purchase a few minutes later, Blake considered what he might tell the girls to hide the nature of his meeting. Unable to decide, he tabled his scheming for later and focused on the box in the seat beside him as he drove the last few miles to the shop.

Arriving at the familiar building, he smiled at the number of cars in the parking lot, noting happy people exiting Spell-bound. Business had grown daily since their reopening; a welcome sign that things were looking up for them despite his brother's interference in their lives. Parking on the side, he grasped his package firmly to crumple the top and hide the contents until he was ready to present it to his girlfriend.

Entering, Blake's gaze swung the arc of the sales floor. A few patrons were looking over their new selection of crystals.

Others were shopping the bookshelves, and a couple were at the register where Karen rang up their purchases. "Where's Sarah?" he asked when she finished the transaction.

"She's not feeling well today," Joseline informed him, joining them from the back. "I've got her on the couch in the office with a cold compress."

"And what are you doing here?" Blake teased. "Oh, let me guess. Here for your mid-day visit?"

The two women played along, exchanging a quick kiss before Josee informed him tartly, "No, silly. I'm here to set up that display we talked about."

"Oh, right. The candles." He chuckled. "Ok, go tinker with it and I'll go check on my girl." He crinkled the packaging as he strolled to the back, rehearsing how he would present it to her.

Opening the door quietly, the darkness of the room enveloped him. "Baby, are you ok?" Genuine concern thickened his voice.

"I ate something horrible," she whined as he cut on the desk lamp, which bathed her in soft light. Her back to him, she faced the cushioned seat, her knees drawn up in an awkward fetal position. "I've thrown up twice since we got here this morning. Once in the trash can."

"Aw, honey," he soothed, taking a knee to lean over her. "I brought you something."

"You knew I was sick?" She sniffed, squirming to face him.

"Not exactly. I had a hunch." He kissed her forehead, checking for fever. "Here. Go pee on this and let's find out if I'm right." Judging from her condition, he strongly suspected his brother had not been lying.

"What's this?" she asked, sitting up to accept the package.

"It's a test," he explained. "Take it in the bathroom and open it. The box says you pee on the stick and we get the results without having to wait."

Sarah eyed him doubtfully. "We've only been at it a few weeks. You think you have super sperm or something?"

"Just go pee." He laughed at her as he stood, then helped hoist her to her feet. "I'll be out front helping with all those customers."

Returning to the floor, Blake gasped. "Where'd everyone go?" Only one of those who had been shopping remained, and she sat in their ring of chairs pouring over one of the spell books.

"They found what they needed and left." Karen shrugged. "At least they were here."

"And they made purchases," Joseline added. Stacking her wares on a small square table, she held her breath as if it might knock them over. Holding up her hands, she waited for them to topple over. When they didn't, she exhaled loudly, then stood up straight. "There. Thanks again for letting me put a few in here. Our place hasn't really seen any in-person sales since last year."

"You're welcome. We—"

"How'd you know?" Sarah shouted, stomping in from the back and cutting him off. Waving the stick at him with her right hand, she planted her left firmly on her hip.

"Know what?" Karen asked, surprised to see Sarah's obvious rage.

"He bought me a test." She presented the device to their co-owner. "I'm pregnant," she announced flatly.

"You're what!" Joseline pivoted to face her. "You guys weren't using any protection?"

"No. We..." Sarah fidgeted, not sure she was ready to face this news, especially in the middle of the bookstore.

"We've been trying to conceive," Blake finished for her, claiming the stick to inspect it.

"Yes. We've decided it's time," Sarah agreed. "But I didn't get sick until after we got here..." She pointed at Blake, "...without you, so how did you know?"

"And why are you trying to have a baby now?" Joseline demanded. "Your brother is about fifteen steps ahead of us. This can't possibly be the right time to start a family."

"Jos." Karen caught her hand, tugging at it. "I'm sure this isn't really our business."

"We're a coven, aren't we?" Josee scowled at her. "That makes it our business."

Sarah tapped her foot, crossing her arms over her chest. "How did you know, Blake?"

His eyes flicking between the three of them, Blake suddenly felt relieved most of the customers had gone. "My brother told me," he confessed, the words tumbling out in a rush.

"Your brother? And how did he do that? Telepathy?" Sarah bit angrily.

"That's the errand I had to run this morning. I went to visit him," their magister explained.

"You went to visit him!" Joseline and Karen shouted in unison.

"What kind of stupid are you?" Josee added. "The man is after us, and you go pay him a social call?"

"Hey, I had my reasons," Blake shot back, his voice rising to meet her irate tones. "And I don't have to explain myself to you. I'm in charge here."

Staring at the instrument, Karen sighed. "I have to agree with Jos, this is bad timing."

"Well, I didn't think it would happen this fast," Sarah lamented, recalling they had talked about it the night they had arrived in Virginia scarcely a few weeks before. "I mean, who succeeds at getting pregnant the first month they try?"

"Apparently, you do," Joseline bit, displeasure radiating from her. "What did Morc say?"

"He asked when she was due."

"No, about us. About the shop. The coven. The curse we transferred from Ezamay to Garrett," she pressed.

"We didn't really talk about any of that," Blake pushed back. "I wanted to tell him that we saved May, but he didn't seem to care. Then he told me about the baby." And he had threatened him as he was leaving, but Blake made sure to skip that part.

"And that's it?" Karen asked doubtfully.

"That's it." Blake shrugged, confused by Sarah's reaction. "I thought you would be happy."

"Why would I be happy?" Sarah exploded. "Josee's right! You *are* an idiot, going in there like that. What did you expect to gain from it?"

"I had my reasons. And again, I'm not inclined to share them with you." Across the room, the bell on the door rang as a couple entered the shop. "We have customers. Let's talk about this tonight, after I get home. Right now, I've got some paperwork to take care of, and then I have a meeting with an old friend."

"That's great," Sarah fumed. "You run off while we run the store."

"Yeah, you run the store." He stood at full height, towering above her. "You guys are part owners. What did you think, it would run itself?"

"Maybe we should hire a cashier or two," Karen suggested, her voice quivering at their argument. "Right now, we need to cool it. We can't afford to run people off with the bickering."

"Exactly." Blake pushed past his girlfriend and stomped back to his office, slamming the door behind him. Staring at the pliable surface she had vacated, he grimaced. "I'm sorry, Baby," he muttered to the empty room. He wasn't sure what he had expected from the moment they learned of their success, but what had happened today certainly wasn't it.

## TWO

## Auntie Up

---

BLAKE HID in his office until three, then ventured out front. Thankfully, another lull had settled in, and the two women busied themselves cleaning and restoring order to the disheveled sales floor. "Wow. That must have been some rush." His voice carried across the open space but neither girl responded. "I guess Josee is back at the Broken Match?"

"Yup," Karen clipped as she adjusted their display of crystals and amulets. "We need an espresso machine and a coffee pot."

"What for?" Blake demanded. "You want people to actually hang out here?"

"Yes," both responded in unison.

"We discussed it while you were sulking," Sarah informed him tartly. "We voted, two to one. We want to set up a little coffee bar and sell drinks so people will feel more comfortable here." She still hadn't looked at him.

"I guess you're still mad," Blake observed more quietly. "I get it. I think we'll need a permit to sell food items, but we can make it work." He looked around the room, noting their new additions since taking over. The only real space remaining was the seating area, and without that, what would be the point of a coffee bar? "What were you thinking as far as placement? We don't have a lot of room left. And we will need someone to man that counter unless you want to go self-serve."

Sarah straightened from her book sorting to glare at him. "I figured you would put up more of a fight."

He sauntered a few steps closer to her. "I feel like shit, Baby." He held his palms up, as if to surrender. "I don't want to argue. This is supposed to be a happy day for us."

"Then don't play games with me," she snapped, returning to the shelf of tomes she had been tending. "Go have your meeting and we'll talk about it when you get back."

"I'll be late, so you guys will have to lock up. Leave the till in the safe and I'll count it for you in the morning. I'll see you at home." Deciding against a parting kiss, he let the order fall flat as he pivoted for a hasty exit. Outside, he paused, the afternoon sun beating down on his upturned face. "Women."

In his car, he blasted the radio as he drove across town, using his fingers to drum on the wheel to release his tension. Cutting it off as he pulled up out front of Madam Demore's place, he grimaced at the sign over her door. Hesitating in his seat, he briefly considered how long he had known the woman and how many times he had actually asked for a reading. He'd probably be able to count them on one hand. He could pretend he was there to collect his key to the shop, but he knew better. If anyone could help him make sense of the chaos, he hoped she could.

Climbing out of the car, Blake squared his shoulders, hoping for a confident air. Opening the entrance, he stood just inside and allowed it to close behind him, giving his eyes a chance to adjust to the dim light of the candles. To his surprise, a young blonde sat behind the counter on a tall stool, a laptop open before her. "Where's the Madam?"

"Hi, Judoc!" The girl greeted him warmly, as if they were old friends. Closing her device, she beamed. "Are you here for a reading?"

"Hannah?" he breathed, stunned by her beautifully tanned appearance. It had been nearly a decade since he had seen Madam Demore's great niece, and a flood of memories tumbled over him, none of them pleasant. "I'm surprised your parents allowed a visit," he mumbled too low for her to hear.

A huge fight had torn a rift in the Demore clan, and the old woman's family had cut her out of their lives, moving away suddenly and leaving her alone in Boston. Matilda Demore had no children of her own, so she had pretty much been on her own ever since Blake had known her, especially these last few years. He had never asked what the tiff had been about, certain she would have said if she wanted him to know. Of course, she never had, nor had she asked him to check in on her from time to time, but he still did.

"Yup, it's me!" Hannah held her arms wide, presenting herself to him for inspection.

"Oh, my! You're all grown up." He shuffled his way closer. "What are you doing here?"

"My great niece is searching for her place in the world," Matilda informed him, joining them via her beaded curtain.

Blake stared at the mystic, a confused expression twisting his puckered lips. "That's nice, I guess."

"Yes, it certainly is. I figure my crazy Auntie Matilda can help me out with that!" The girl giggled playfully, wriggling on her seat. "I graduated a few weeks ago, and of course my parents had my future all planned out." She rolled her eyes, her hands flopping around as she spoke.

"But you didn't like the plan," Blake surmised.

"Nope. Who wants to sit in a stuffy office all day?" She shrugged. "Not this girl. Therefore, I'm not going back to California."

Blake chuckled at her, thinking of Sarah and Karen, who were only a year or two older. "I guess you want an outdoor job?"

"Oh, no, not necessarily. I just don't want to be stuck at a desk all day. That's what I'm doing right now. Searching for something fun that will keep me busy. When I find the right job, I'll be all set," Hannah informed him smugly.

"You'll find something," Matilda agreed, joining them at the counter. "Boston is a booming place. You never know when the right position will open up." She glanced at Blake, hinting for him to make her great niece an offer.

Grinning, Blake understood perfectly, and if he were honest, he knew they could really use her. Plus, she could be trusted. That was huge when looking for help at a place like Spellbound. "Well, if you need something in the meantime, we could use a hand at the shop," he suggested, smoothing his hair along the back of his neck. "We've been busy, and the girls want to put in a coffee bar." He laughed at the thought of it. "You know anything about coffee shops?"

"Are you kidding? I was a part time barista back in Santa Monica. I can certainly help with that if Auntie says it's ok." She clapped her hands, her excitement at the prospect genuine.

"That's fine by me," Madam Demore crooned. Her mission accomplished, she left them to take her seat at a round, cloth-draped table, her large glass ball positioned before her. She held up her hand, indicating for Blake to have the one across from her. "Judoc?"

Blake pursed his lips, studying her for a moment before flicking his gaze back to Hannah. "Come to Spellbound in the morning and we'll fill out your paperwork. You can start tomorrow."

"Thanks, Judoc." She opened her computer, ready to return to her surfing.

"Actually, please call me Blake," he said more quietly. "I know Madam Demore still calls me Judoc, but I haven't gone by that name in years."

"Ok, Blake. Thank you!" She didn't look at him this time, already lost in the world of the web.

Turning to the matron, he crossed the narrow room and took one of the empty chairs. "What makes you think I need a reading?" he asked sweetly.

"What makes you think I didn't know you changed your name?"

His jaw dropped in surprise, his confident air slipping. "Hey, it's not a big deal. You can call me Judoc. I don't mind."

"Still clinging to the past," she observed. "If you wished to be called Blake, you need only to have asked."

He inhaled deeply, studying her. "I envy your talent," he confessed quietly.

"And I yours," she replied. "But I am not a witch, like you. My gift will never compare to yours."

He shook his head, a smile spreading over his tired features. "It's been a long day, Madam Demore. Just when I think I have everything under control, I get thrown a curve ball." He indicated her crystal. "Ok, I want a reading. I want you to tell me about my son."

She waved her hand above the smooth glass, searching for their target. "Oh, he's a handsome young man. Yes, I see him quite clearly." She watched intently, interpreting the scenes for a long moment before she added, "His mother believes you are unaware of his existence. Are you planning to take him from her, or will you continue to watch from afar?"

Blake's grin disappeared, and he swallowed. "My son isn't born yet. Sarah and I just found out today that she's pregnant." He blinked at her, hoping she had been viewing some image from the future, but her comments about the boy's mother caused him to doubt it.

Matilda's jaw grew tense. "The child I see is alive and well, Judoc. Perhaps eight years old. Maybe ten."

"That can't be." He gasped, glancing at the young woman who shared the room. "I'm very careful with my seed. If I had gotten some wench pregnant, I'd know about it!" he bit, anger coloring his flesh with a bright pink hue.

"Careful you might be, but the boy does exist." She wiggled her fingers, as if refocusing the view. "I would offer to show him—"

"You know I see nothing within your magic crystal," he snapped, leaning towards her slightly. "I will hear no more of this. Tell me about the child Sarah and I share." He paused, clenching his teeth as he considered the unexpected news. "Never speak to me of this other boy again. His existence would be...impossible. I refuse to believe it."

Her mouth hanging open, Madam Demore curled her fingers into a light fist, then lowered her hand. "I see no other child, Judoc. Are you certain she has conceived?"

Leaning back in his chair, Blake felt as if he'd been punched, his red flush fading. "Yes, I'm sure." He blinked rapidly, tears welling in his clear blue orbs before a glimmer of hope came to him. "Even the best seers don't know everything." He sat up straight, slapping the table gently with an open palm. "Perhaps he is just obscured for some reason. Or maybe he's a girl! That could be why. I'm asking for the wrong thing."

"I see nothing, girl or boy." Her features sank, the curve of her lips forming a small pout. "I'm truly sorry, Judoc. I wish there were more I could give you on this matter." She glanced at her niece. "If you wish to withdraw your offer, I'm sure she would understand."

"It wasn't a payment. The job is hers if she wants it," Blake bit sharply. Covering his mouth with a hand, he leaned against it for a moment, contemplating the situation. He didn't ask for readings often, and this was precisely why. "You never tell me what I want to know."

She chuckled at his muffled observation. "That's not how seeing works."

"Yeah. So it is." Standing, he bowed slightly towards her. "How much do I owe you?"

"Your money is no good here, Judoc." She smiled up at him. "But aren't you forgetting something?"

"The key." He snapped his fingers at the remembrance. "I'll need it back. And thank you again for tending the store while we were away. Hopefully we won't need to be gone again."

"Did all work out well then with your endeavor?"

"Indeed." He sneered at their having beaten Morcant's curse. "We saved Josee and Meri's mother, and bought ourselves some time. Hopefully it will be enough."

"Watch yourself, Judoc. Your brother was dangerous when you were on good terms," she warned, her brows drawn into tight crinkles.

"Don't worry, Madam. I'm always careful." He backed away, waving to Hannah. "I'll see you in the morning," he called loud enough to break her trance.

"Yes, sir!" the girl replied crisply, returning the gesture as he disappeared out the door.

## THREE

## Closing the Deal

BACK IN HIS CAR, Blake slumped in his seat, his head resting in his left palm. He still had a meeting with Jason, but for now he just wanted to sit there. The madam had not been kind in her reading, leaving him with only questions and doubts.

After a few minutes of pouting, the coven's magister pushed himself up straight. "Can't sit here all day," he muttered to himself. "Time to man up and take care of closing the deal with that guard. Otherwise, this morning's visit was a huge waste of time."

Putting the car in gear, he sped away, arriving at the bank just before closing. Making his withdrawal, he grinned at the masked clerk, considering that eventually things would get back to normal. Maybe. "Can I get a plain white envelope from you?"

"Sure." She smiled behind the covering as her gloved fingers slid it across the counter and under the new plexiglass divider between them. Some things would never be normal again. "Anything else?"

"Nope. Have a great day." He gave her a small wave as he turned to go.

Once safely back inside his vehicle, he placed the money in the simple white pouch and added the note he had so carefully penned earlier in his office before sealing it. He had planned the meeting well, but at the moment he couldn't wait to get to the bar and have a few drinks.

As soon as he entered the techno club, Blake cringed. The stiff beat of the music put him on edge. Taking a seat at the bar, he looked around, realizing it was early as there were only a few patrons milling about the place.

"What'll you have?" The barkeep, a heavyset man with a full beard had a face that would scare small children.

"Just a Heineken," Blake replied, trying not to stare. To himself, he muttered, "Man, I hope this guy doesn't make me wait too long in this dump."

Almost two hours and a six pack later, Blake looked at his watch and considered that the guard might not show. The room had filled, and the noise level made his head swim. He'd done his best to avoid Madam Demore's reading from earlier that afternoon, but no matter what path he considered, it always led him back to the foul news she had given him: a son he refused to accept and another that was only a shadow. A hope or dream that might not come true, despite what the pregnancy test had revealed.

"Hey." Jason interrupted his thoughts, taking the seat next to him.

"About time you showed up," Blake growled. Hoisting his green bottle, he finished it off. "I was contemplating leaving any minute."

"Yeah well, something came up." Jason didn't apologize, and his shouted excuse fell flat between them.

Pulling the crinkled envelope out of his back pocket, Blake laid it on the bar, giving it a few taps with a stiff digit.

"I'll take another," he called to the ugly man serving people down the way and giving his empty a wave at him.

"I'll have the same," Jason added, picking up the thin package and placing it in his lap, away from prying eyes. "I wasn't expecting anything tonight," he added to the man next to him. "You must be desperate."

"It's just a down payment," Blake replied matter-of-factly, leaning towards him so he didn't have to scream. "There's also a number inside. And instructions. Don't call it. Text anything that happens, but don't use my name or my brother's."

The bartender placed their drinks before them. "Anything else?"

"We'll let you know." Blake folded a twenty-dollar bill in half lengthwise and offered it to him.

"No problem." The beast snatched the creased bill and strolled away, shoving it in his pocket.

Jason watched the burly guy, pursing his lips before taking a huge swig. Placing the half-empty bottle on the flat surface before him, he swiped away the residue. "Think he's stealing from the till?"

"Who cares." Blake cut his eyes over at his new minion. "You got any questions?"

"You're awfully confident," Jason groused. "Technically, I haven't agreed to help you."

"Then what are you doing here?" Blake demanded.

"I've got some things at home. Expensive things that I can't really afford right now," Jason explained, then shrugged. "This is a line I've never crossed before."

"Hey man, I didn't ask for anything other than info." Blake sat up straight and looked around at the chaos. "Are you a regular here?"

"Hell no." Jason laughed, also observing the mob around them. "I picked it to avoid seeing anyone I know. You?"

"No. I don't hang out in bars, especially ones with such terrible music." Blake chuckled as well, his paranoia ebbing, but only a bit. "My brother puts me on edge."

"He's an evil bastard," Jason agreed with a nod, then a few more swallows of brew.

"Why'd you say that?" Blake asked in surprise.

"I only had one friend at the prison," Jason supplied, peeling the label on his beer. "A few months ago, he got the invitation to work for Mor—"

Blake cut him off. "Don't say his name."

"Fine. For M. But my buddy turned him down. A few weeks later, he had a crash on his bike. Bad. He hasn't been back at work since."

"But he lived?" Blake blinked at him, his thoughts churning. He took a nip, glancing around again.

"Yeah, he's still breathing. But I don't think it was an accident. And he won't ever be right," Jason put it bluntly.

"Smart man. Very observant." Blake toasted him, then tipped the bottle to empty it. "There's three grand in the envelope."

"I didn't ask you for money yet," his new crony insisted.

"So?" It's yours. Keep it. Consider it a gift. If you decide you have anything to tell me, just follow the directions. Like I said, I'll make it worth your while."

"I don't want to end up like my friend." Jason glared at him, waiting for a reassurance that wouldn't come.

Instead, Blake stood to go. "I'll see you around." Turning his back, he picked his way through the crowd and headed for the door, his ears ringing when he made it out into the warm night air of summer.

## FOUR

## Packed and Ready

"Thank you, Boo," Meri said cheerily, then ran her fingers over the tape he had applied to her box.

"You're welcome, Boo." He leaned in to kiss her gently on the lips. "Have we packed enough for today?"

She giggled. "Almost." She surveyed the collection of boxes that had slowly filled their living area. "I had no idea we had accumulated so much stuff."

"Ha ha. I had quite a stash before you got here," he reminded her while stacking a few cartons against the wall to clear a path.

"Yes, you did!" she affirmed as she moved to help him, then paused, her hands frozen in midair.

Noticing her stiff form, Rider glanced at her face. "What's wrong?"

"I don't know," she whispered. "I feel odd. Something's happened to one of the girls."

Rider straightened his tall frame, then faced her squarely. His gut twisted at her use of magic. "I'll have to get used to that, I guess. Can you tell what? Or how bad?"

Merideth stood frozen, her breathing shallow. She had always had her intuitions but learning to control them had never mattered until she met Blake and the members of their coven. Pulling her crystal from her pocket, she glared into it. "I can't see them. I need to call."

"Then we're done for the day," he stated flatly. Stepping into the kitchen, he pulled a bottle of wine out of the fridge and plucked a glass off the rack. Picking his way between their belongings, he took his favorite seat on the balcony, all the way to the right and away from the sliding glass door. The air hot and humid, he left the gap open for her to join him when she had sorted out the details of her latest premonition.

The sun hung low over the building across from their flat. Pouring himself a portion, he enjoyed the sounds of evening, only catching a word here and there as Meri made her call inside. When she finally came out, the ball of fire had completely disappeared, only leaving faint light and shadow on the street. Joining him, glass in hand, she waved it at him, indicating her desire.

"Well?" he asked. He accepted the crystal and poured her serving before handing it back, placing the bottle on the small table between them.

"They're ok, I guess." She sat heavily in her designated spot in front of the door. She sipped before she added, "Sarah's pregnant."

Rider gasped, almost dropping his drink. "Now?"

"Yes. Apparently, they wanted to start their family," she informed him quietly. Meri tapped the side of her beverage with a long nail. "She didn't think it would happen so fast. I'm not sure if she knows how she feels about it yet."

"Hmph," Rider grunted. "One can never tell about those things, I guess." He returned to enjoying the quiet, knowing all he needed to about the situation in Boston.

"I'm worried about her, Boo," Meri said softly. Flicking her gaze over at him, he seemed annoyed rather than concerned.

"Yeah, she's a good kid. It's a shame Blake has such a strong influence on her," he muttered.

"He loves her," she defended. "And that's not what I'm talking about."

He cut his eyes over at her, taking another large drink. He had agreed to join their merry little coven, but that didn't mean he liked it. "We'll be there in a few days. You can't really do anything until then. Are they ready for us?"

"Yes, she said they have one of the guest apartments all ready. It's downstairs, so we will have our privacy."

"Thank God." Rider polished off the glass and reached to pour another.

"Karen is moving in with Josee."

Rider finished the pour with a scowl, placing the bottle back on the flat surface with a thud. "That's a bit premature, don't you think?"

She sighed heavily, swirling her glass. "It doesn't matter what I think. Or you, dear Boo. They are both adults. Karen says they are kismet."

"Pfft. Rubbish." He took another swig.

"Are we going to eat or were you planning to drink your dinner?" She changed the subject, knowing that he was going to Bean Town with her, but his heart would always belong to NOLA. That's why he had insisted on keeping the studio open and renting out their flat rather than sell it; he planned to return at some point.

"I haven't decided," he clipped, not looking at her.

"Well, I'm going to put something on. You can join me when you're ready."

Slipping back inside, she left him to enjoy one of his last remaining evenings in good old New Orleans.

"That was sweet of her," Josee observed as Sarah hung up the phone.

"Yeah." Sarah sniffed, staring at the device. "Your sister is very...thoughtful."

"I bet she doesn't like us moving in together," Karen observed, arriving next to them in the hallway outside her empty room.

"She's fine with it, or at least she sounded fine," Sarah corrected.

"I'm sure it's Rider who will have the problem with it," Joseline agreed.

"Rider has a problem with everything," Karen pointed out, and the trio giggled. "It'll be fun to watch him and Blake go at it when they get back. I think Rider is an easy target." Stepping through the doorway, she sighed. Her eyes darted over the sparse furnishings; only the bed and dresser remained. She'd had her doubts when they moved in, but now she felt a little sad to go.

"You ready, Babe?" Sidling up behind her, Jos slid her hand up Karen's back, urging her to speed things along.

"You're leaving now?" Sarah whined from the doorway. "I thought we'd have one more dinner before you go."

"We'll be back for dinners, Sarah." Joseline rolled her eyes. "She's moving across town, not across the state."

"I know, but still..."

Karen looked at her best friend, saddened by the droop of her shoulders. It had been rough, finding out she was pregnant that morning and losing her bestie the same night, officially at least. She had been staying over at Josee's house since they returned from Virginia. It only made sense to make the move permanent.

"Sorry, love," Joseline interrupted their silent conversation. "Karen and I have a double date. We're meeting Bert's new girlfriend tonight."

"Ah, that's right." Sarah nodded. "Hard to imagine him in a relationship."

"Be nice," Karen commanded. "He's still Josee's brother, more or less."

Sarah sighed, wishing it were less.

"Mew." Caly rubbed against Sarah's leg, and a tear spilled onto her cheek.

"It would be cool if I could talk to her like you do," she suggested to Joseline.

"Why? I thought you guys didn't like each other," Jos replied crisply.

"That was back when she was a person." Sarah laughed, wiping away her drops of sadness. "I like her fine now that she's a cat."

"We should get going," Karen cut in. "We'll barely have time to unload the car before they arrive at the house."

"True," her girlfriend agreed. "Bye, Caly," she called, stomping towards the stairs.

Picking up the cat, Sarah followed closely behind. When they reached the porch, she shoved her into Karen's arms. "You should take her, too." Scooping up her food and water bowls, she presented them as well.

"Why would we take Caly?" Karen asked in surprise.

"Because Joseline can talk to her." Sarah opened the door and placed the dishes on the passenger side floorboard. "Go on. She'll be happier."

Karen scrunched her nose doubtfully. Glancing at her partner across the top of the car, she shrugged.

"We'll take her," Jos agreed, climbing behind the wheel.

Sarah waved as they pulled away, then went back inside alone.

## FIVE

## Empty House

BLAKE FELT a dull ache form in the pit of his gut as he pulled up in front of the dark mansion. He'd been gone longer than he intended, and the sight of the lifeless windows couldn't be right. Mounting the steps, he paused, noting Caly's dishes no longer sat in their place next to the door. Inserting his key, he flung open the portal.

"Sarah?" he screamed, panic tainting his voice. "Karen, where are you guys?"

No response. He flicked on a lamp on his way by, headed for the kitchen. There in the dim light, a hunched figure sat at their table, a bottle and glass on the flat surface before her.

"Sarah?" he panted, relief flooding his scattered thoughts. "Baby?" He could make out enough to recognize her, but her lack of reaction frightened him.

Leaving the light off, he crossed the few steps and knelt before her. Covering her knees with his hands, he gently squeezed. "Sarah, what's going on?" Seeing the label on the bottle of wine on the table before her, he glared at the glass. "Have you been drinking?"

"No." She lifted her chin and stared at him with hollow

eyes, the pale light from the other room exposing her tear-stained cheeks. "I decided it wouldn't be good for the baby."

"That's a relief," he stated firmly. He didn't specify which, that she hadn't been or that she had at least considered their child. "Why are you sitting here alone in the dark?" He pivoted, indicating the front of the house. "And where are Caly's dishes?"

"Karen's gone," Sarah moaned. "They took the last of her stuff. I sent the cat with them."

"Oh." Blake's lips puckered, confusion replacing fear. Glancing around, he faltered. "You want to make dinner with me?"

Her puffy, swollen eyes blinked at him. "I'm not hungry."

"Aww, Baby, you need to eat." He stood, leaving her. "Light's coming," he warned before flicking the switch.

Covering her face, she protected herself against the flood of illumination. Her long red locks hanging next to them, she held an eerie appearance beneath the glow. Grabbing a chair, he scooted up next to her, placing a strong arm across her shoulders.

"How about grilled cheese and tomato soup? It's easy, fast, and one of your favorites," he suggested.

She blew between her fingers in a disgusted fashion, slowly lowering the digits to allow her eyes to adjust to the light. "Are you going to force me to eat?"

"Well, no, but you must be hungry." He stood, collecting the unopened bottle and glass to return them to their proper places. Selecting a couple of cups, he placed them and a half-gallon of milk on the table. Pulling out the cheese and butter, he put a pan on for the sandwiches and another for the soup.

A few minutes later, he ladled the steaming broth into bowls and placed her sandwich on a small plate, cutting it into fourths for her. "There you go, sweetness."

Taking his seat, Blake gnawed at his sandwich, then slurped a few spoonsful. Watching her, he noted that she seemed frozen, unable or unwilling to move to join him. "Boy this was an exciting day," he enticed.

"Exciting? Not how I would describe it," she challenged. Picking up a triangle of bread and cheese, she inspected it. He had put two slices in, making sure they were gooey between the browned toast. Perfect, indeed it was just the way she liked it. Tears in her eyes, she swallowed. Not ready to take a bite, she opted for the beverage, sipping a bit of the milk, then wiping at the film on her upper lip with her forearm.

Blake grinned at her attempt. "I have some good news," he informed her amiably. "I found a clerk to help on the sales floor."

She cut her eyes up at him, peering through the strands of hair that hung in her face. "That was quick."

"Yeah, I stopped by Madam Demore's to pick up my key. Her great niece was there, fresh out of college."

"And she aspires to sell books with her education," Sarah quipped, her lips curling into a twisted grin.

Blake chuckled, encouraged by her surliness. "Well, it won't be permanent, but it will give us an extra pair of hands until she finds something in her field."

"And what, pray tell, is her field?" Sarah tore the sliver of sandwich in half and took a bite. Like magic, the flavor exploded inside her mouth. "Oh my God." She had been hungry.

"You know, I didn't ask." He finished off his own bread and cheese, then the soup. Sitting back in his chair, he waited for her meal to also disappear.

When she was done, Blake moved to collect their dishes. "Was that enough or do you need something else?" He placed the load in the dishwasher, giving her time to decide. When the chore was complete, he turned to find her slouched over the table, her head on her arm, completely zonked.

"Oh, wow." Laughing at the spectacle, Blake scooped her into his arms and carried her out of the room, barely managing to flick off the lights with his awkward cargo.

"What?" Sarah twitched, mumbling in her sleep.

"You're fine," he whispered, making it to the couch and resting her on the cushions. Any other time, he would have gone for the stairs, but he didn't want to risk a fall with their precious package growing inside her. Instead, he collected a pillow and blanket from the closet to make her comfortable. Tucking it around her sock-covered feet, he grinned, giving her thigh a light pat. Leaning over her, he breathed in her scent, his heart fluttering inside his chest as he kissed her forehead.

Taking a seat in the chair, Blake kicked off his shoes, then hoisted his shirt over his head to expose his hair-covered chest. Sitting back in comfort, he glanced at his pack of cigarettes and then over at the girl. He never would have thought twice about lighting up around her, but so much had changed. Snatching up the container and the lighter, he quietly opened the front door to let himself out into the night air.

Sarah woke some hours later. Staring at the coffee table, her nose scrunched, she grunted, "What the hell?" She hadn't had anything to drink, so she knew she hadn't passed out on a bender. Sitting up, the blanket fell from her shoulder, and she noticed she'd left a small drool spot on the pillow.

Next to her feet, the lamp cast a soft light across the room. She stretched, inspecting the space in wonder as if she had never been there before. In the chair that formed a corner with the end table, her man lay hunched over and slept against his arm.

"Aww, Baby, what did you do?" she asked him quietly, not

intending to wake him. Obviously, he had brought her out and let her rest. His tenderness brought tears to her eyes, as if she hadn't cried enough the day before to run them dry.

"Hey," Blake whispered, his blue orbs blinking at her.

"Hey yourself," she replied, standing quickly and claiming his lap. Her knees pressing against the cushions on both sides, her hair cascaded around them as she kissed him.

Holding her, Blake opened himself to her, loving the feel of her hands massaging his muscled chest. "Are you ready to go upstairs?"

"Why? We have the house to ourselves," she purred. Lifting her own tee over her head, she dropped it to the floor.

Sliding his fingers beneath the elastic of her bra, Blake teased the edges of her breast. "A rare treat," he growled.

She freed the clasp, and the covering fell away, exposing her scrunched nipples. Standing, she undid the button and zipper on her jeans and fought her way out of them. Down to only her socks, she whined, "You're still dressed."

"Not for long," he assured. Pulling the front of his pants open, he lifted his ass and forced them down without bothering to stand. His cock hard, it stood straight up when he sat back and she eagerly straddled him, taking it inside her.

"Ow, oh," she groaned, holding herself up from fully penetrating her wetness. Her breath catching in her chest, she gasped, whining, "Oh, shit."

"Come down," he begged, his arms clasping her bare hips.

"I...can't." She gasped. "It hurts," she confessed, forcing herself to take him, the motion almost agony.

"What? Why?" He held her in place, not ready to give up on front-room sex. "Is it the baby?"

"I don't know," she confessed, catching her breath. "I've never been pregnant before."

He lifted her off him, pushing her back. "Lay on the

table," he commanded. Spreading her legs, he inspected her labia and fingered the opening. "You look all...bruised. It's all purple down here."

Her hand resting on her belly, her fingers splayed across her warm flesh. "Is it really in there?" she wondered aloud.

"It must be." He shrugged. "You've never looked like this before. What if something's wrong?"

"I feel ok. If it were wrong, I think I would be bleeding or something."

He nudged the pea of her clit with his thumb, giving her shivers. "You like that, Baby?"

"Uh-huh." She massaged her belly, enjoying the moment with him.

Leaning in, he continued to tease her with his tongue. Taking turns, he used it and his fingers to massage and then explore the cave of her womanhood. Then he inserted a long digit into her ass, finger fucking it gently. "You are so hot, Baby."

Pushing her along, Blake pleasured her with his mouth, his fingers working her as her urgency grew. Her bare flesh sweaty, it stuck to the wooden surface as she arched against him, groaning.

"That's it, sweetness, cum for me." He sucked against her clit, then flicked it rapidly with the tip of his tongue until she squealed, her hands grasping at his hair. The waves undulating through her, he didn't stop until she lay still. Panting, he blew cool air against her hot flesh. "Enough? Or do you want more?"

"I want more," she agreed, fighting to sit up. Pushing against his chest, she got him into the chair and reclaimed him, his fullness within her. The pain gone, she breathed in deep breaths of relief.

"Are you ok?" he asked, unsure what to do next.

"Yes, it's fine now. Just be still," she commanded, taking over for him. Using her legs, she rode against him, taking him in deep strokes. Kissing him, she could taste her juices on his lips. "You're so good to me, Baby," she whispered.

"I love you, Sarah," he replied. "I don't say it enough, but it's always there."

Arching her back, she pushed harder against him, enjoying the feel of his cock inside her. "Tell me when I'm not fucking you. Right now, I don't care," she growled.

Grabbing at her shoulders, he thrust up against her. If she didn't want to hear it, maybe he could show her. A moment later, he yelped. He squeezed, trying to stem the cascade as his groin grew tight, then gushed with a burst of release. "Shit!"

"Let it go." She moaned, thrilled by the quiver of his body beneath her.

He groaned loudly, his hands gripping her forcefully. "You bitch, I wasn't ready," he teased. He pressed his face against the flesh of her belly and chest as she lingered over him, trying to hold her still.

She giggled, moving enough to torture him with chills. "Well, I guess we'll just have to do it again, then. The house is empty, and that means we can fuck wherever we want, as many times as we want." She bent to kiss him, her red waves tickling his flesh.

"You bet we can," he agreed, massaging her bare back firmly. Pushing her to stand, he got to his feet, then shoved her onto the sofa. "Once we're done in here, we'll move to the kitchen. Give that table a try."

She cackled at his silliness, spreading her legs and making room for round two.

## SIX

## From a Distance

BLAKE STROLLED up to Spellbound the following morning, a light whistle emanating from his puckered lips. Opening the door, he let himself in, then locked it behind him, as they wouldn't be opening for a few hours. He had left Sarah at the house to enjoy a bath, so he would count the till as promised and have everything ready for her when she arrived.

It pleased him to see how well Sarah managed the shop. Karen was a partner, of course, but she had never taken the same interest in the business as his girlfriend had, and he figured it was only a matter of time before it was just the two of them. Opening the safe in the office, he removed the money bag, noting the weight of it.

"Wow, sales were good." He placed it on his desk and went over to start the coffee pot before he got to work.

A short time later, he placed the bag back in the safe so that he could run it to the bank once the girls arrived. Taking the starting till and his cup to the front, he had just finished setting up the register when the bell clanged and Sarah let herself in.

"Good morning," she sang cheerfully.

"Good morning, missy," he replied, grinning at her. "How do you feel?"

"Sore," she snipped. "Last night was fun."

"You like having the house to ourselves," he teased.

"Yeah, I guess. But it won't last. I talked to Merideth last night, and they should be here early next week."

"Oh, that's good, though. We need to work on getting that pendant off Joseline's neck, and I really want the gang all here for that."

"I was thinking we should do it in Virginia," Sarah suggested, hiding her purse under the front counter. "We should include Ezamay as well, and I'd like to know how Garrett is doing."

"Well, surely he's doing ok. He's only been carrying the curse a few weeks, after all." Blake moved to the sales floor, tidying up here and there where things had been left out of place.

"Hey, guys!" Karen called breathlessly, the door closing behind her. "Sorry I'm late! We had a full evening with our dinner guests." She paused, pulling up the blinds and flicking on their open sign. "I'll stay late tonight if you want."

"Karen, you're a partner. You don't need to make excuses," Blake reminded her, shaking his head.

"Oh. Right." Karen nodded, dropping the conversation to go get herself a warm cup of morning brew from the back.

"She's a little scattered," Sarah observed, glancing out the front. "And our girl is here. Gosh, she's quite lovely, Blake," she teased.

"Yeah, and I've known her since she was a toddler so she will always be a kid to me. She's actually about your age, or close to it." He opened the door to greet her. "Come on in, new girl. This is my girlfriend and one of my partners, Sarah." He indicated the redhead, giving her a wink.

Holding out her hand, the blonde announced, "Hi, Sarah, I'm—"

"Hannah!" Karen exclaimed from the back entrance.

Blake blinked at the girls with his jaw dropped in surprise. "You guys know each other?"

"Yes, this is Hubert's girlfriend," Karen replied crisply. Holding out her coffee so as not to spill it, she gave their new clerk a one-armed hug.

Sarah watched her, doubtfully, recalling the night they had given Hubert the boot from their coven meeting. The same night they found Joseline. Glancing at her mate, she could see he wasn't any more thrilled at the news than she was.

"What are you doing here?" Karen asked, unaware of the conflict simmering around her.

"I'm your new salesclerk!" Hannah beamed, obviously pleased with her new position.

"Oh!" Karen took a step back, sloshing the hot coffee. "Damn it," she cursed. She placed the mug on the counter and fumbled for a rag underneath. "That's wonderful news. We really need some help around here. It'll start getting busy here in about an hour and will be steady until we close this evening."

Hannah had wandered off, eager to have a look around. Watching her, Blake pursed his lips, then called to her, "Hey. Let's go get that paperwork filled out. Then we'll let Karen show you around."

Sarah held her breath as she watched them go, then let it out in a loud huff once they were out of earshot. "Are you really that into her or is this just a show?"

"What do you mean?" Karen asked, completing her cleanup.

"I mean, we decided that Bert was an outsider. What are

you doing getting all chummy with him and his new girl-friend?" she hissed.

"Well, for starters, we aren't chummy. And secondly, Hubert is still Joseline's brother. They grew up together, so we may have held our meeting and conducted some business without him, but he's still part of her life. And part of mine by extension. If there's a problem with that, I can always go and help at the Broken Match. I'd like to spend some time over there anyway and get to know more about it." Karen raised her chin defiantly as she spoke, daring Sarah to push her.

"Fine." Sarah shook her red mane, meeting her best friend toe to toe. "She's only temporary anyway, so it's not worth fighting over. I'm going to inventory the crystals and get an order ready. Have fun showing her around." She tossed her locks a final time as she turned and stomped over to the amulet display.

Karen rolled her eyes as she wobbled her head, attributing Sarah's moody disposition to her delicate condition. "I wonder if there will be nine months of this," she muttered to herself. Deciding to take some measurements, she set about plotting their new coffee bar while she waited for Blake and Hannah to finish in the back.

Several hours and over a hundred customers later, the bell on the door rang as Hubert himself entered the store. "Special delivery!" he called, wheeling his dolly up and placing a stack of boxes at the end of the counter.

"Bert!" Hannah squealed, hopping over to kiss him. Her cheeks flushed, she glanced around to see if they were a causing a spectacle before leaning against him and shoving her tongue down his throat.

"That's not very professional," Sarah observed to no one in particular.

"Aww, lighten up," Karen replied. "I think they're cute."

"Right. Cute," Blake mocked, rolling his eyes and lifting one of the boxes. "I'm glad we made our little arrangement, Bert. Your sister's candles are a real hit." He placed the carton next to the half-empty display and prepared to restock it.

Bert's arms still around his girl, he half-heartedly agreed. "Yeah, I guess. I'm not sure she should have done that. Now we have to share some of our profits when we could have had them all if we were selling out of our own shop."

"They weren't selling out of your shop," Blake growled. "They're buying them here on our reputation."

"Pfft," Hubert huffed. "Whatever you say." Lowering his face to Hannah's he said more quietly, "Wanna get out of here, Kitten?"

"I can't do that." She giggled. "It's my first day. I'll see you tonight though."

"Party pooper." He kissed her quickly, then dropped his arms. "I'll have more for you tomorrow."

"See you," Blake called, waving at him without actually looking up from his stacking. He had just finished the last box when the phone rang.

Beating him to it, Hannah answered it while grinning at him, "Spellbound Book Emporium." She listened for a moment before her features fell. "Oh no."

Blake's brow furrowed and he stepped closer, attempting to hear. A male voice barked from the other end, but he couldn't make out the words.

"Oh no!" Hannah repeated more forcefully. "Ok, let me tell Blake, or do you want to talk to him?" She listened a moment, then held out the phone. "It's someone named Rider," she announced. "He thinks I'm Sarah."

Taking the device, Blake paused, considering what to do next. His new clerk's reaction to the call didn't bode well for what the other man had to say. "Hold on a sec," he commanded into the receiver. Placing the call on hold, he dropped he handset into the cradle and strolled to the back where they could speak in private.

At his desk, he punched up the call. "Yeah."

"Blake," Rider snapped. "We've got a problem, man."

"What kind of problem?" Blake had already imagined they were going to back out on coming to Boston, so he was braced for whatever news would come next.

"Someone torched my studio," Rider informed him angrily.

"What?" Blake gasped, not as ready for the news as he thought. "When?"

"Last night. Burned it to the ground."

"Where's Meri? Are you guys ok?"

"We're fine. She's at the apartment, getting some rest. We've been talking to investigators all day, after being called to what's left of my building around three this morning."

Blakes mind leapt to what he and Sarah were doing at about that time. "I'm sorry. What do the police think?"

"They're dead set that it was intentional. The bad news is Merideth and I are stuck here until we get this figured out," Rider lamented. "Don't look for us in Boston next week."

Blake's eyes narrowed as he considered the news. "Yeah, I got you. You guys be careful."

Rider ended the call abruptly, and Blake stared at the phone before hanging it up. "What an asshat. He probably blames me for this," he muttered.

"Who blames you for what?" Sarah asked from the doorway. She had followed him off the floor, curious what kind of call had him running to the back.

"Rider. He said that his art studio burned down last night." His face expressionless, or as close as he could get it, he hoped the news wouldn't upset her.

"They aren't coming, are they," she said quietly, taking a few steps into the room. When he didn't reply, she pushed, "It was arson."

He pressed his lips together tightly. "It wasn't an accident, if that's what you mean."

"I mean, someone is going through a lot of trouble to keep them in New Orleans," she bit tartly. "And the new girl you hired just happens to be Bert's new squeeze?"

"What are you implying?" he asked, looking past her to ensure they were alone.

"That I don't like this." Her chin dimpled and her bottom lip trembled. "Is Meri ok?"

"She's fine, honey." He came around the desk, meeting her with a firm embrace. "Look at you and your pregnant self. Got your emotions all in an uproar." She shook in his arms and he knew she had broken into actual tears. Stroking her hair, he soothed her, rocking her side to side. "It's ok, Baby. They'll get it sorted out and be here as soon as they can."

Pulling away, she sniffed, wiping at her damp cheeks. "I hope so. You were at Madam Demore's yesterday. Did she give any indication this was going to happen?"

Blake stepped back, hesitating. "Baby, you know I don't ask her too many questions."

"Yes, but maybe she offered something." She plucked a few tissues out of the box on the desk and dabbed her eyes. "With the baby and everything, you weren't even a little curious?"

Blake shoved his hands in his pockets. "Ok, you got me. I asked, but I can't share what she said."

"Why not?" She stared at him with wide eyes. "Was it bad?"

"No, it was confusing. Like always." He yanked his hands

free to fold his arms across his chest. "She never says anything that makes sense until after it happens."

"So, what did she say?" Sarah snapped, tired of his dancing around.

"I can't tell you that," he said gently. "If I tell you, that makes it real and I'd rather just forget it."

"Oh. She did tell you something about the baby," she accused.

"Not exactly. She said she couldn't tell me anything, and I'd just as soon not try to guess what that means," he huffed, turning to leave her.

"Wait!" She grabbed his arm, preventing his departure. "What about Meri and Rider? We can't fix Joseline until they're here."

"We may not be able to fix her at all," Blake countered quietly. Grasping her hand, he squeezed. "We need to be strong right now, sweetness. We have a few more hours before the shop closes, and then we can talk more about it tonight. When we get home." Pulling away, he left her there, ready to bury himself in his work and forget about the coven's mounting problems for as long as he could.

## SEVEN

## Boston Awaits

---

Ending the call, Rider slipped the device into his pocket. Glaring through the office's window, he could see three men in suits standing in a larger room filled with desks. He didn't know what they were discussing, but if he had to guess, he would say it was his answers to the latest round of questions.

Around the men, people in and out of uniform scurried about. Some carried papers, others talked on phones or radios. Everyone seemed in a hurry.

Finally, the huddle ended and Bryan Forsyth returned to his office. Taking the cushioned seat behind his desk, he folded his arms across the flat surface and stared at Rider. "Mr. Bradshaw, we've done all we can for today."

"Ok, so when do we get some damn answers?" Rider demanded.

"Well, the investigation is still under way. We have located the other artist who shared your studio. He's out of town, so we'll be questioning him when we can arrange it," the detective explained.

"Great," Rider clipped bitterly. "But Robert didn't have anything to do with this either."

"That will be determined. I'm sure you're right," Bryan agreed, turning up his palms. "For now, we're sending you home. I know you're in the middle of a move to Boston, but we'll need to speak to you and Merideth again either tomorrow or the next day."

"Don't worry, we aren't leaving until this is settled," Rider growled.

Nodding, Forsyth stood, indicating the open door. "We'll let you know, then."

Rising, Rider offered his hand despite social distancing, but was prepared to withdraw it should the other man protest. When the officer accepted it, he gave the man across the desk a firm shake. The familiar action felt good and boosted his confidence that they would, in fact, get to the bottom of the disaster in short order.

Arriving home a brief time later, he found Meri curled in their bed, the drapes drawn to keep out the late afternoon sun. Pulling off his clothes, he slid beneath the covers next to her. Draping his arm across her, he sighed heavily.

"Any news?" she asked quietly.

"None. They have no clue what happened. Only that the place went up like a tinderbox. I'm sorry I woke you."

"Don't be. I wasn't resting well without you here," she confessed. Rolling beneath the arm, she faced him, laying her hand against his bare chest. "We should call the girls and Blake to let them know what's happened."

"I thought of that and took care of it just a bit ago. We'll get there when we get there. Boston can wait."

"Hmm. Ok. Goodnight, Boo."

He raised his head, planting a kiss on her forehead, then nestled in to get some rest.

It was dark out when the couple awoke hours later. Their stomachs empty, Meri could hear his growl in the darkness.

Rolling onto her back, she stared at the ceiling, then whispered, "Are you awake?"

"Yup. It's two in the morning, so we slept through dinner and it's not time to get up yet." He chuckled, feeling better after the much-needed sleep. "Are you up for a snack?"

"I guess we could make an early start of it. We still have packing to do." She slid out of the covers and stood, taking her robe off the door. "You want a full meal or just a bowl of cereal?"

"Let's start with the cereal and go from there," he suggested as he searched for the clothes he had dropped on the floor hours before.

As the couple ate, Rider postulated about how the fire could have been started. "There are only a few people who hold keys to the building, and with the alarm not going off until the blaze started, it looks like an inside job."

"I'm going to call Mother and Daddy first thing in the morning. I should have done it yesterday, but I was too tired when I got home. Do you think we should call your father?" Meri asked.

"What for? He isn't really into my life here. I'm not sure what good it would do." Rider took a noisy sip from his cup. "But I do know who we should contact!"

"Who?" Merideth's eye's drooped, despite his excitement. She propped herself up with a stiff arm and tried to appear awake and interested.

"The tuath. The one Dad sent us to a few years ago. She's a seer, like you. Maybe she can tell us something about the fire or who might have set the blaze."

Meri chewed her lip, considering the plan. Finally, she said quietly, "I still want to go to Boston."

"We can't leave," he replied sharply. "Forsyth said they will need to talk to us again in a day or two."

"Fine. After that, I'm buying a ticket and heading north," she stated firmly. "I have a bad feeling the fire was set to keep us here and I won't be made a pawn in someone else's game."

"You think Morcant somehow arranged this?" he asked incredulously. "Come on, Meri. The guy's in prison. There's only so much he can do from there, no matter what our fearless magister thinks." He stood, as if to close the subject, and poured himself another cup of coffee.

"Such a disbeliever," she taunted. "Blake was right about a good many things. I'm going to call him in the morning as well and get his thoughts on this."

"Yeah, you do that," he grumbled. "I'm sure he'll appreciate your hero-worship."

"Where's that coming from?" She sat up straight and glared at his back.

"Well, he did help save your mother and all." Rider shrugged, making light of his disparaging remark as he reclaimed his chair. "You admire him for that, I'm sure."

"Yes, I think he is a very wise and even powerful witch. As is his brother. They have a hundred years of practice, so I value his opinion," she detailed, her voice rising as she spoke.

"Hey, don't get all defensive. I'm sure they will be glad to have you there, and I can handle whatever the investigators need. So don't worry. Buy your ticket and go, and I'll finish up everything here and join you when I'm able."

Meri watched him slowly raise the cup to take a sip, considering if he ever would in fact join them. "You're still not sure about becoming part of the coven."

"Stop using your gift on me," he growled. "I don't like it."

"I didn't need second sight to pick up on your mixed feelings, Boo. You've dragged your feet every step of the way. The packing has taken twice as long as it should have. If you don't want to go, you should say so now," she insisted.

"Hey, I said I would go. Stop pushing me." He stood, the chair grating loudly across the floor as he shoved it back. Leaving the cup in the sink, he added, "I'm hitting the shower."

"Leave some hot water for me," she called to him as he disappeared down the hall.

Merideth exited the airport in Boston three days later. She had brought two large trunks of clothing and personal items, as well as a small carry-on along with her purse. Stopping at the curb, she spied a bench and laid claim to one end of it. Sending a text, she announced her arrival. A moment later, Blake's red Camaro pulled up in front of her.

"Wow, I wasn't expecting more than a couple of suitcases," he teased as he joined her.

"They are suitcases," she countered. "Sort of." She looked around anxiously, then said more quietly, "I brought everything that I valued. I don't plan on going back to NOLA."

"Oh." He studied her, his hands on his hips. "Did you two have a fight?"

"Not exactly. I'm just not sure he wants to be here." She blinked rapidly, avoiding his cool blue stare. "He says he has to take care of things there, and I understand that."

"He'll come," Blake predicted, bending over to inspect her luggage. "I think we'll fit one of these in the trunk with the smaller bag and toss the other in the back seat."

"Ok." She smiled up at him, relieved he hadn't made a big deal of things. "I never thanked you for standing up for me."

"When did I do that?" he teased, hoisting an oversized pack and dropping it in the trunk of his car.

"That day we first met you. Rider kept insisting that we

were non-practicing. I went along, but it was so hard. I felt like I was dying inside. I don't know what I would have done if you hadn't allowed me to be myself."

"I'm sure you would have figured it out." He tossed her carry-on in next to the larger piece of luggage and slammed the trunk lid. "Nice. It fits."

"Now you have to get the other one in the back."

"Piece of cake." He folded the seat, then lifted the trunk, placing it against the door frame before mumbling something she couldn't quite hear. Giving it a shove, it slid in and fell over into the back seat.

"Did you just shrink my bag?" she asked in surprise. Leaning over, she peered in at it.

"I have no idea what you're talking about. Get in and let's go," he called as he jogged around the car and climbed behind the wheel.

"You did shrink my bag," she squealed, twisting in her seat to inspect it. "How'd you do that?"

He cut his eyes over at her, not bothering to explain.

Righting herself in the seat, she asked, "What about the stuff inside? Is it like super compressed, or is it smaller as well?" She smashed her hands together, demonstrating her query.

Blake shook his head, chuckling. "You have so much to learn, Meri dear. I'm really glad you decided to join us."

"I didn't have much of a choice," she said quietly. "I want to know things. I want to use my talent and not feel ashamed of it."

"You should never be ashamed of who you are or what you can do. I'm sorry Rider made you feel that way." Blake gripped the wheel more firmly, angered that she had been treated so unjustly.

"It's not his fault. His father wasn't a good role model."

"No, Thaddeus certainly has his flaws," Blake agreed. "And you will learn much, Meri dear. As much as you want to know." He glanced at her, smiling at their new member. When they arrived at the house, he pulled her bag out of the back and righted the size.

"Why didn't you wait until we got it upstairs? That would have made more sense," she observed.

"It weighs the same, either way," he pointed out. "I'll teach you the spell some time and you can practice. For now, leave it, and I'll come back for it once I have this one safely inside."

"You're such a gentleman," she praised. "What would I ever do without you, Blake Korrigan."

EIGHT

## Good Company

---

Bursting out the front door, Joseline grabbed her sister and squeezed her tightly. "Oh my God, I'm so glad you're back safely." Looking past her, she scoured the driveway, only finding Blake as he carried her sibling's oversized bags to the steps. "Where's Rider?"

Returning the embrace, Meri blinked her damp lashes. "Hi, Sis." She stepped back, inspecting her near twin. "He wouldn't come. He says he has to take care of the business in New Orleans before he can."

Her mouth gaping, Josee struggled to hide her talent, her sister's pain ripping at her heart. "I'm so sorry, Meri. I know this must be hard for you."

"Immensely." The younger girl coughed a laugh. "Let's get my things settled and then we can talk."

"Your suite is this way." Sarah relieved her of her carry-on bag and led the way through the living area, past the bathroom under the stairs. At the back, a passage turned to the left, one that would likely go unnoticed by most who entered the mansion.

Following, Meri paused at the long hall. On the right, a

door led to the outside, and on the left, three doors evenly spaced across the expanse. Turning into the first one, a small efficiency apartment greeted her, with a two-chair dinette in the center of the room. Along the left-hand wall, a tiny fridge, two-burner stove, and a single sink. On the right, a wall that only jutted from the edges a few feet, leaving a large opening between the two rooms. In the gap, a curtain hung to the side which could be used to obscure the double bed. "How charming. No potty?"

"It's this way." Sarah crossed the divide and pointed at the door on the far wall. "And this is your closet." She indicated a wardrobe to the right, tucked inside the short wall that separated the bedroom from the kitchen.

"Wow. This is nice. I guess." Meri looked around at the cramped space, not sure what to make of it. "You said these were servant's quarters?"

"In the past, they have served as many things," Blake informed her, delivering her bags. "This house has been in my family a few centuries."

"How ever did you get both of these trunks into your car?" Karen asked, inspecting the parcels.

"He shrank one of them and shoved it in the back seat," Meri informed them with a chuckle. The other three girls turned to stare at him with wide eyes.

"You can do that?" Sarah asked breathlessly. "Why didn't you tell us?"

"A witch only spends the magic that they must. Flaunting our powers only leads to problems with those non-magical beings who dominate our world." He left it at that, turning to go find dinner. "I'll be in the kitchen," he called over his shoulder.

"He never ceases to amaze me," Merideth breathed. Taking a few steps, she opened the bathroom door. "It's a pass through." The toilet, sink and shower all lined the left-hand wall. The right held a door, with cabinets on either side. Opening this portal, she found the outside exit straight across from it. "We can come and go this way?"

"Yes, it goes to the back garden, which is also accessible via the kitchen and patio. If you park in the alley, you basically have your own entrance." She beamed at the design. "I think you will be comfortable here."

Taking the hallway, Meri opened the last door, discovering an identical apartment behind it, one that would share her bathroom if occupied. "How quaint. Still, it could be worse."

"Are you hungry?" Joseline asked, joining her to inspect the other apartment, then dropping an arm across her shoulders. "We bought steaks and potatoes."

"I brought salad stuff as well," Karen added. "Some of us like greens."

"I'm famished," Merideth confessed. "We were packing for weeks, and then there was all the stress with the fire. I haven't been taking very good care of myself lately."

"Well let's go have some dinner then, and you can get some rest," Jos declared, releasing her hold to lead the way.

A couple of hours later, the group lingered over the meal, which had done their morale wonders. Observing the faces around her, Merideth felt more relaxed than she had in weeks. Had Rider been there, it would have been perfect.

"So, tell us about this bag shrinking," Sarah demanded, glaring at Blake as she swirled her glass of grape juice and pretended it was wine.

"There's nothing to tell." He chuckled at her behavior, and her questions. "I can do lots of things. With magic, the possibilities are endless."

"But we don't understand why you hide it." Joseline

joined in the interrogation. "If we are so bloody powerful, why are we the ones cowering in secret?"

"Because mortals are not the only dangers we face. Not only are we vastly out numbered by them, but other witches would definitely have a say."

"Madam Demore doesn't hide hers," Sarah pointed out tartly.

"Ah, but Madam Demore is not a witch," Blake replied crisply. "If there is any magical blood in her line, it is quite diluted."

"So, Hannah isn't either," Karen surmised.

"Then how does she read fortunes?" Sarah snapped. "You had her read mine, and the baby's."

Blake's cheeks took on a deeper hue. "She has certain talents. Gifts, if you will. She's a seer, which is rare among mortals. It is also the cause of her separation from them, even though she is not truly one of us. Those who know of her talents shy away from her. Even her own family has broken ties with her."

"But Hannah is here to follow in her footsteps," Joseline pointed out. "She seems rather happy to be a part of our world."

Blake nodded. "Before everything fell apart, we had several mortals within our coven. My brother liked having them around, as they are easier to persuade to do our bidding. Or *his* bidding. I'm not one to force my will on others, if I can help it."

Merideth scrunched her nose, sipping from her crystal. "That's mighty big of you, magister. Everyone wants their share of the power. And the spoils," she pointed out meekly.

"Speaking of spoils, do we have any fresh ideas about Morcant?" Karen asked bluntly.

Merideth cringed at the mention of his name, and Joseline

flinched. "What's wrong, Meri? Did something else happen in NOLA, besides the fire?"

"No, nothing happened, really." Meri drummed the side of her glass with her nails. "I didn't sleep well the whole time we were gone."

"Nightmares," Blake stated flatly. "What did you dream?" He sat back in his chair, expectantly waiting for the details.

"Nothing specific." She shrugged. "Different things, all ending in being chased or falling from tall buildings. Your typical night terrors."

"Were we in any of them?" he pushed. When she only looked around at the others, he grimaced. "Your powers are still young. You will learn to control them in time."

"I hope so," she agreed. "I was really scared, but I feel better being here."

"Our numbers give us strength." Blake took a few short sips, offering a smile. "What was in the dreams, Meri?"

"We were all in them at some point. He was in all of them, I think. Or people who were helping him." She hesitated, glancing at Sarah. "I saw Caly as a girl, once. She had long blond hair. And another named Tinia."

Blake, Sarah, and Karen all reacted to the name, the girls emitting a gasp in unison. Calmly placing his elbows on the table and folding his hands to lean on, Blake soothed, "That's fine, ladies. She's a seer. Viewing portions of our past is normal."

Merideth swallowed, unsure if she should press the issue. Instead, she lamented, "I worry about Rider being alone down south. And my parents. Even you girls living across town," she confessed, glancing at the couple.

"What, you think we should all pile in here?" Joseline clipped. Taking a gulp of her libation, she dismissed the thought. "No thank you. We are close enough where we are."

Merideth averted her gaze, that having been exactly what she had thought the moment she saw the second apartment. She played it cool, still hoping they could be convinced at some point.

"Maybe." Blake cut his eyes over at Jos. "How's business at the Broken Match?"

Slowly returning her glass to the table, she stared at him. "It's slow. What are you getting at?"

"Bert dropped off a delivery to us every day this week. Your candles are flying out of our store. I think you should abandon your storefront and join us at Spellbound," he suggested.

"What?" Joseline squealed. "I have no intention of moving in on your business, Blake," she snapped.

"It would only be temporary, I assure you." He glanced at Karen and Sarah. "I want to open the rooms under the shop for our use as a coven."

"Oh, no!" Karen whined.

"Do we have to?" Sarah seconded.

"Yes, I believe that we do." Blake glared at them, hoping they wouldn't go into detail as to what transpired there.

"Those rooms are cursed," Merideth pointed out for them.

Sharing the gaze with her, Blake shook his head. "Then we will hold a cleansing. I would say meeting upstairs was fine, but with Hannah and Bert hanging around, I feel that might be unwise."

Sarah stared at him, dumbfounded. "If you didn't trust her, why did you hire her?"

"Because we need someone who can run the shop when we are busy with other things," Blake snapped. "I'm the magister. I don't have to explain my choices to you. Any of you."

Joseline could feel the rage welling inside him. "We all

know and respect your position, Blake," she pointed out calmly. "If you say we need the rooms, then we will make them ready." She absently rested her hand on her chest, feeling Morcant's stone beneath the cloth of her shirt.

Noting the action, Blake pursed his lips but said nothing of it, opting to change the subject. "How about dessert?"

"We got a chocolate cake," Sarah sang, springing from her chair to fetch it. "Double Dutch."

"Oh, I love chocolate," Meri and Jos said in unison, then giggled. "We have so much in common, Sis," Meri added.

"Then let's have no more talk of my brother and our struggles. We'll have time for that after the cake. And a good night's sleep," Blake commanded, hoping they would heed his word and give it a rest for the remainder of the evening.

## NINE

## A Little Magic

THE FOLLOWING MORNING, Blake left Karen in charge of the store with Hannah to help her while the rest of the girls gathered at the top of the stairs. The landing was quite large, and Meri peeked into the office, which opened to the left, recalling the first time she visited the shop. Blake sat at the desk, finishing the morning paperwork before they got started.

Standing next to her, Joseline took her hand and gave it a squeeze. "Don't be scared," she whispered. "You're with us, so nothing is going to happen."

"What makes you think I'm scared?" Meri retorted, giving her a sideways glance. "Sarah's a little afraid. Maybe you should give her the pep talk."

"Hey! I heard that." The redhead glared at them angrily.

"Nothing to be afraid of," Blake announced as he joined them. "I've made a pot of coffee, so we work for two hours and then we'll take a break. It's a bit dank down there."

"Is it already open?" Sarah squeaked with her face scrunched.

"No, I closed it up after only a bit of straightening once the whole incident with my brother happened. It's been sealed since the pandemic hit as we had no need of it, until now," he explained as he led them down the stairs. Looking over his shoulder when he reached the bottom, the girls hovered behind, almost in a clump. Laughing out loud, he quipped, "Would you guys relax? Your impression of that cartoon dog and his shaggy friend is hilarious."

"Har-har." Sarah moved away from the others, but only a few inches.

Still holding hands, the sisters giggled. Neither of them had ever been in the basement, but they each sensed the darkness on the other side of the door and wanted no part of it.

Using a key, Blake opened the portal and it swung wide, revealing a pitch-black chamber. Flicking the lights on at the switch, the fluorescent bulbs flickered as they fought their way to life.

"Man, it stinks in here," Joseline observed. "You should have aired it out once in a while."

"Honestly, I never intended to use it again," Blake confessed, working his way in. Dust coated the tarps they had used to cover the furniture, with a splattering of cobwebs to add contrast here and there. Pausing halfway in, he stopped. "Someone's been here."

"What do you mean?" Sarah asked, pulling on a pair of gloves.

He pointed at the floor. "I see where they walked, and that shelf of books has been disturbed. See how the dust and webs aren't even across it?"

"It looks like some are missing," Joseline agreed. "Who had access besides you three?"

"Who knows. With the pandemic, we didn't come here very often. We were officially closed for months." He tiptoed over to inspect the shelves. "They definitely took some of his tomes. Three or four by the looks of it."

"What's in them?" Meri asked, her voice shaky.

"Just spells and stuff. Nothing over the top that I know of," he replied, squatting as he continued to probe. "The worst part is what this confirms."

"Someone's really helping him," Sarah concluded.

"Yes. My brother couldn't have done this, so it had to be one of his minions in here snooping around," Blake verified. Dusting his hands together, he stood. "Ok, we need a trash can, the broom and dustpan, and a few masks wouldn't hurt."

"Bleh, masks?" Joseline whined. "Haven't we had enough of those?"

"Well, you only need one if you don't like breathing dirt," Merideth teased. "Where can we find those things?"

"I'll go up and gather what we need. You guys start putting together the boxes I brought down earlier." He indicated the stack still out in the hall.

"Ok, guys," Joseline said airily. "The sooner we get this done, the sooner we can get out of here."

"I don't know," Merideth countered, looking around the spacious area. "Now that we're down here, this place isn't so bad."

"You weren't here before." Sarah clicked her tongue in disgust. "I don't view this place as a hangout, and probably never will."

"Give it time," Meri assured, her lips curling into a slight grin. "We'll wipe away every trace of Morcant and make it our own."

"You bet we will," Joseline agreed.

Above them, Karen and Hannah had started their day by reshelving books and restocking the candles and crystals before they got busy. Working her way over, Hannah hovered close to the other girl. Eventually, she asked, "Why are they working on the basement? I thought you guys were putting in a coffee bar."

Karen laughed anxiously. "We are. But the basement will be more of a hangout for employees."

"Oh, like a break room."

"Yeah, like that." Karen beamed at the idea. She wasn't certain that Hannah would ever be welcome there, but it made a good cover story. "But we are definitely going to do more remodeling to get that coffee bar in here. Maybe we can draw up some sketches during our spare time."

"Sweet." Hannah bounced in place. "I love planning things. And Auntie wouldn't let me touch her shop. She said it was arranged the way she liked it."

"You know Merideth is an interior designer," Karen pointed out.

"Shut the front door. Did she go to school in Cali?"

"I think so. She wants to have her own shop someday. She moved to NOLA with Rider, but the pandemic kept her from really getting anything started down there. Don't tell me you are as well."

"I started out in it, but decided it wasn't for me. I changed degree plans and ended up with more of a general diploma. I like landscaping."

"Landscaping?" Karen paused, turning to gape at her. "You went to college to be a gardener?"

"Well, there's more to it than that." Hannah laughed. "I design outdoor spaces."

"Boy, Rider and Meri are going to love you." Karen joined her frivolity, then returned to her stocking. "We better hurry. We won't have time for this once the customers start piling in."

"Yeah. You guys are way busier than I remember it being back when I was a kid."

"You used to come here?" Karen hadn't known that.

"Yup. Auntie had a table in the corner. She performed readings. I loved to watch her crystal ball, but I'm pretty sure it's all a hoax. I never saw anything inside the glass. But Judoc and Morcant helped her get her start. When she was popular enough, she opened her own shop. It's the one she has now," the blonde provided.

"That's nice. I'm glad she's doing so well."

"Oh, that was before the pandemic. Everyone is hurting now, but things are picking up over there just as they are here. I think being locked in and scared got people interested in the occult," Hannah observed. The door clanged and she looked up. "Welcome to Spellbound," she greeted, then whispered to her new friend, "And so it begins."

"Go take care of them. I'll finish this up quick," Karen promised, watching her swish her hair as she went. "Yup," she added to herself. "It seems more people than ever are looking for a little magic in their lives."

"What do you think?" Blake asked anxiously as Karen viewed the room from the door.

"It looks like she hates it," Joseline observed, crossing her arms. "After all our hard work."

"I didn't say that," Karen countered, her voice trembling. "I died here. You'll have to give me a minute to rearrange my schema of this place."

Around the room, nothing of the old space remained. They had gutted it, hauling everything up the stairs and out to the dumpster Blake had rented and placed in the back of the shop. Once the walls were all that remained, Merideth had gone to work, revamping the divided room into two sections, one that would function as the break room, and the larger room behind it for private meetings.

"I think it works well," Meri chimed in, proud of her work. "The art on the walls will please Rider, I think." She had selected seascapes, bringing out the cool colors in the décor.

Taking a few tentative steps, Karen swallowed. "I'm glad you guys understand. And thank you. I don't see anything that was here before."

"We removed it all," Blake pointed out. "I trashed everything except my brother's tomes, and those aren't stored here."

"Where did you hide them?" Joseline asked quietly.

"Someplace safe." He winked at her, not ready to divulge the location.

"You think he can hear you through my necklace, don't you," the girl accused, her hand patting it through her shirt.

"I didn't say that. But it does concern me that you still wear it." He watched her motion. "Do you even realize that you do that?" He imitated her.

She jerked her hand away from the bulge beneath the cloth. "Well, it's not like I can take it off. If I get more than a few feet from it, I feel physically ill. But no, it's just a habit. I'm not sending signals or anything."

"We need to work on getting it off you," Blake said simply. "I'll feel better once that's done."

"We all will," Karen agreed, still watching around her as if the new furnishings might attack her. "I'll come down here for meetings and stuff, but please don't expect me to be relaxed or make this my hangout."

"You'll get used to it. Meri said the decorations would have a calming effect." Blake turned, ready to head up the stairs. "You guys take your time. I'll watch the front for the afternoon and let you all settle in."

Following him, Joseline called, "What about my candle shop? You promised you would go over our sales numbers this week."

"Well, come on then. We'll sit at the counter and look them over between customers," he suggested. Stopping by the office, he gathered the spreadsheets he had printed earlier that morning.

Pulling up a stool next to him, Joseline glanced around the busy sales floor. "Is it always like this?"

"Pretty much," Blake confirmed.

"It wasn't like this before. The changes you guys have made really improved your traffic. I can't wait to see what the coffee bar does for you," she praised.

"Yeah, the coffee bar." Blake hung his head for a moment, shaking it slightly. "I'm never going to hear the end of that."

"You don't want one? They're great! You put in a little Wi-Fi access, and people will never leave." She giggled, thinking of the possibilities.

Blake only grunted, flipping open his sheaf of papers. "These are the sales reports from the last two weeks." He offered them, giving her a better view.

Her eyes roving over the numbers, Joseline gasped. "This can't be. How did M & J's ever keep the doors open?"

"Morcant wasn't interested in sales, or profits for that matter," Blake explained, keeping an eye out around them. "The store was a front."

"A front? For what?" She couldn't believe her ears. "He and I were pretty close. He always seemed legit to me, and he bought enormous amounts of candles from me. You don't think he was reselling them, do you?"

"I have no idea what he did with them. Burned them, maybe. The store gave him access to people, and that's what he treasured most." Blake folded the pages and greeted the pair of ladies who had walked up. "You two doing all right?"

"We're fine," one of the women replied, placing her pile of trinkets on the counter. "Will these bring us good luck?"

"Absolutely," Joseline assured, placing each in a velvet pouch for them, glancing between them. "I have one I keep hidden." She patted the stone under her shirt but stopped short of pulling it out to show off.

"Wonderful." The other woman beamed, accepting the package as Blake handed over their receipt.

"Thanks for coming to Spellbound." He grinned, his straight white teeth making him perfectly swoon-worthy.

"Bye-bye." The women whispered to each other as they left, one of them looking over her shoulder before the door closed.

"You add to the experience," Joseline pointed out when they were gone. "Morcant's smiles would make most people's skin crawl. Yours is more...dreamy."

"We are very different people, he and I," Blake agreed, watching the women climb into their car through the glass door. "I want to be successful here. I want the store to thrive and turn a profit for many years to come."

Opening, the pages, Joseline sighed. "I used to feel the same way. Only now I realize that having a candle shop on my own will likely never get me there."

"You could stay here," he offered, turning to face her. "We used to rent space to Madam Demore. We could do the same for you."

Joseline met his gaze, her lips pressed tightly to prevent their trembling. "You are an amazing man, Blake. I feel so blessed to have finally met you."

"You've known me for years," he pointed out with a smirk.

"No, I knew of you, and what I knew was mostly untrue.

It's only been in these last few weeks since my brother and sister arrived that I've seen the real you. Thank you. I'll put together a business plan and figure out what I can afford to pay," she declared.

"Sounds good." He took the pages and stepped back, offering her the register. "You want to run it for a while?"

"I can." She smiled warmly at him, the sparkle reaching her eyes as it seldom did.

Leaving her to the chore, Blake headed for his office to put away the paperwork and then to check on the girls below.

## TEN

## Mystics and Seers

STILL WEARING HIS BATHROBE, Rider sat in his favorite chair on the balcony of his New Orleans flat. Unshaven, he made a pitiful sight, having not been out of the apartment in two days. Tilting the bottle in his hand, he finished off the last beer in the house. Glaring at it, he belched, then smacked his lips.

Merideth had left for Boston exactly eight days before. He had told himself on the first day that he wouldn't need to think about her. Everything would be fine without her there. At first, he kept busy, finishing off the packing and following leads with detective Forsyth.

By the fourth day, he'd had nothing left to do. He bought a case of beer and told himself he would enjoy his bachelorhood while he could. "Yeah, this is the life," he mumbled, fully aware that no part of sitting outside drinking at ten in the morning seemed fun, and it hadn't in years.

Looking over his shoulder, he glared at the painting. He had started it the day she left. A surprise for her when she got home. Somehow, he couldn't imagine taking it to her in Boston. "Pretty lady," he toasted, raising the empty towards it.

He still couldn't believe he would give up his home there in New Orleans for her. Or at least he planned to. He hadn't yet, and therefore he could always change his mind.

Standing, Rider lumbered inside, his bare chest and legs peeking out of the open front of the untied robe. Crossing the living area, he glared at the boxes stacked there, waiting to be opened and all his things put back in their rightful place. In the kitchen, he yanked the door and stared into the empty fridge.

His heart grew heavy inside his chest. "What if this is real?" he asked the appliance. "What if I have to *go* to Boston to be with her?"

He closed the door, recalling the days he had spent there with her, protecting her from an unseen enemy. Their early days had been filled with danger, followed by months of being thrown together during the pandemic mania. He hadn't been sure where they stood, but he felt he might fold with her gone.

Suddenly, an idea came to him. "The tuath." He had suggested going to see her about the fire before Merideth left town. He still could. And if she happened to give him advice on other things, well, so be it.

Pivoting, the robe flowed behind him like a cape as he scampered down the hall, dropping the flannel cloth on the floor. Pulling on his jeans and t-shirt, he shoved his feet into his shoes and headed out the door.

Taking his bike, Rider arrived at the shotgun house a short while later. Parking on the street, he looked up and down the block, considering the woman might not live there anymore. Deciding there was only one way to find out, he sauntered up the path to the steps, and finally rapped lightly on the door, which opened before he was done.

Surprised, Rider took a step back, allowing his target to join him under the awning. "Hello," he chirped anxiously.

"Well, if it isn't Rider Bradshaw. It's been a few years," she observed, quietly closing the screen door behind her. "My little one is asleep in the front room." She indicated the seats off to the side, "I'm assuming you're here for a visit."

"You remember my name." He smiled, wiping at his face, only then recalling his disheveled appearance.

"Of course. Thaddeus is an old friend. Are you in trouble again?" she asked, noting he looked to be on the run once more.

"Maybe," he confessed, taking the seat on the outside, allowing her to be close to the door. "Someone burned down my art studio, and I was hoping you could provide a little insight as to who might want to do such a thing. I'm sorry, I don't have any books or feathers this time for you to read from."

Sitting in the wicker chair, she smiled at the memory of their last visit. "How did things work out with you and the girl?"

"Oh, they're fine. She's in Boston." He fidgeted, expecting that to be enough. When she waited for more, he added, "We're in the process of moving that way. She's there now, actually, and I'll be joining her soon, I guess."

Her lips twitched as he spoke. Offering him her hand, she waited for him to place his within it. Turning it over, she opened it so she could inspect the palm. "You doubt she is the one."

"Oh, I don't doubt, but it scares me shitless."

Her eyes shot up to stare at him.

"Sorry. It scares me to death," he clarified, causing her to giggle.

"You haven't come to me for answers," she informed him flatly. "You already know them all."

"Then what am I here for," he demanded, tempted to yank his appendage away.

"Permission I think." She ran a finger lightly over his flesh, tracing one of the lines. "You are so desperate to remove yourself from our world."

His lips puckered. "You know my father. What kind of man he is."

"I know we each see those around us through our own eyes. Our perceptions colored by our own experiences. He and I were good friends. I do not know him in the way that you do." She smiled encouragingly.

"I'm not really here to talk about him. I'd rather know about the fire." He swallowed. "Or about Meri."

"The fire is of no consequence. It will only serve its purpose as long as you allow it. As for the girl..." She paused, swiping again. "You have a connection to her that can never be broken."

"Yeah, we share a sister," he blurted, earning another jolted glare. "We aren't siblings," he added quickly, "but each of us has a parent who is also Joseline's parent."

"Oh, Thaddeus," she clipped. "You speak of the child of darkness. The one he shares with Ezamay."

"Yes," he whispered.

"I was the one who told him they could not keep her. Our relationship became strained after that, and we have seldom spoken since. You were never to learn of her existence."

"Well, we found out a few months ago, which is a long story. All of my stories are long, it seems." He laughed to break the tension. "She's great, by the way. Joseline is. I mean, Merideth is too, but she's not my sister. She's my girlfriend."

The woman smiled at his twisted thoughts and rambling tongue. "To choose to marry this Merideth will forever complicate your existence."

"What does that mean?" he snapped, finally pulling his hand away. "Are you saying I should stay here and leave her there all alone?"

She shook her head slowly. "I cannot advise which path you should take. If you want that kind of advice, there are those who read fortunes in the market who would dispense such shallow guidance."

He blinked at her. "I'm sorry. That was rude of me. I know in the end the decision is mine. But I had hoped you could at least give me a hint which option would be, you know...cleaner."

"Remember what I said about your father, Rider. We each see him in our own way. And so it is with your future. What I might call cleaner could be pure torture for you." She held up her hand, indicating his slouched form. "This is all the evidence I am willing to present."

"This?" he asked, running his hands over his shirt and pants. "What's wrong with this?"

"You look tired, Rider. Lost. How long has she been away?"

"Eight days."

She raised a brow at him. "And you have not run to her?"

"I can't go to Boston. I have to stay here until the investigation is over," he snapped, feeling the urge to leave the porch in a dead sprint.

"What if it never ends? Will you unpack your boxes and let her go so easily?" He stared at her, his thoughts churning. "How'd you know all our stuff was in boxes?"

"Oh, Rider." She laughed at him. "What good is it to visit a mystic if you doubt their words?"

Standing, he grunted, "You know, you people are no help. Thanks for your time," he called over his shoulder as he skipped down the steps and climbed on his bike. He was nearly home before his pulse had slowed enough to allow him rational thought.

Parking, he climbed off the seat and stared at the place she had sat behind him too many times to count. "I'm going to lose Meri," he said to himself. "If I don't go to her right now and protect the coven as I promised, they may all die." He could feel it in his gut, and he didn't need a seer to tell him that.

Taking the stairs in twos, he burst into his apartment full of more energy than he had felt in days. Opening his laptop, he pulled up a search, then made the call to arrange for a moving van to pick up their stuff the following morning. Then he called the realtor to inform her they were no longer interested in renting the flat. Instead, it would need to be sold, and the sooner the better.

Finally, going to another website, he booked his flight for the following afternoon. "Hang in there, pretty lady," he said to his creation on his way by, headed to the back of the flat. "Boo's coming!"

ELEVEN

# Rider's Girl

RIDER WOKE up early the following morning. Jumping in the shower, he faced the day with a full head of steam, knowing in a few hours he would have Merideth by his side. If he played his cards right, she would never leave it, and that was enough to push him forward.

Out of the shower, he dressed quickly and then shoved every other stitch of clothing he could find into a suitcase, clean or dirty. He figured they could sort it out when he got to Boston or wash it all. It made no difference to him.

Careful to place the box he had purchased the previous afternoon in his pocket, he touched it often, ensuring it was still there. Throughout the day, he dreamed of different ways he could present it to her. "It's got to be special!" he said to himself time and again.

By the time the truck pulled up out on the street, he had everything packed and ready. Greeting the men at the door, he called them inside. "Everything goes, gentlemen. Furniture, beds. All of it." He figured they would put it in storage until they found a place to buy. "But easy with the boxes, please. Some of that stuff is irreplaceable."

Taking Merideth's picture off the easel, he tucked it inside a large, zippered pouch with handles, intending to take it on the plane with him. Leaving the movers to load their stuff, he took a cab to the police station. Inside, he went straight to Forsyth's familiar office.

"Hey, Bradshaw! Come in," the detective greeted him warmly, then noted his bag. "Going somewhere?"

"Yeah, Boston," Rider clipped. "Meri's already there, and I just can't stay here waiting around for you guys to catch the arsonists or figure out what happened. I have to get to her."

"I'm sorry, but that's not protocol," Bryan stammered. "You really shouldn't leave until you are cleared to do so."

"And I've got that covered." Rider produced a notepad from his pocket. Tearing out one of the pages, he presented it as he explained, "This is the address of the bookstore where Meri and I will be working. Some friends of ours own it. And this is their house. It's a mansion, really. Old money, so the guy is loaded." He nodded in an exaggerated fashion. "You'll find us there. Or you can have one of the locals in Boston swing by if you need us. Oh, and our numbers are both on the back."

Passing the paper over, Rider didn't wait for permission. Picking up his pack, he called on his way out. "My plane leaves at one and the moving truck is packing our stuff as we speak. Hope you break the case!"

Bryan stared after him, dumbfounded. Then coming to his senses, he ran after him. Catching him at the security desk, he gasped for air. "Hey, you know you can't collect the insurance on the building until we clear this up."

"I don't care about that." Rider clapped him on the back a few times. "I care about Meri, and she's in Boston. Take care!" And with that, he was back out to catch another taxi, this time to see a guy at the bike shop across town.

Leaving his bag when he arrived, he paid the driver to wait, then peered around, searching for the guy who owned the place.

"Can I help you?" one of his grease monkeys asked.

"I'm looking for Smitty. Is he around? I'm on a schedule, so I don't have a lot of time," Rider explained, indicating his taxi.

"Naw, you missed him. Won't be back for a couple of hours." The guy spat on the ground while using a red rag to wipe down a wrench. "Can I tell him something for you?"

"He offered me ten grand for my bike. Tell him Rider said it's a deal. I left the key and the title with the realtor, so it's accessible. All he needs to do is wire me the cash, and it's his. Here's my number." He removed another slip from his notepad and handed it to him.

"Ok!" the guy took it, shoving it in his pocket.

"Don't lose that," Rider commanded, pointing at his coated coveralls. "Maybe go put that on Smitty's desk or something."

"Good idea." Turning, the mechanic strutted away, hopefully to do just that.

Back in his cab, Rider barely made it to the airport in time to catch his flight. Sitting in his seat hardly an hour later, he breathed deeply, tamping down his excitement. He hadn't called to warn Meri or the others that he was coming. He wanted to surprise her and hoped she had missed him as much as he had her.

"Can I get you anything?" the flight attendant asked, interrupting his thoughts.

"A Gray Goose martini," he replied. He had never had one, but Meri seemed to like them; so, he would give it a try in her honor. Afterwards, he wished he had opted for a beer, but it had been ok. At least he had tried it outside her presence, so she didn't have to see the awful look on his face when he tasted it.

Landing in Boston, Rider picked up his painting and suitcase from the luggage claim. Gingerly, he opened the precious package to inspect her image. Everything appeared to have traveled safely, so he joined the line for a cab. Soon, he was on his way to Spellbound and so eager to get there he couldn't sit still. Fidgeting, he opened the box from his pocket and stared at the precious gift. "I hope she likes it."

"Is that for your girl?"

"Yes, it is." Rider held up the box, tilting it so he could see.

"Oh, that's a nice one," the cabbie praised. "I'm sure she's gonna love it."

"Thanks. I really hope so." He returned the box to his pocket and closed his eyes in an effort to calm himself.

When they pulled into the parking lot, Rider paid the man and leapt out of the cab, dragging his suitcase and the painting with him. Flinging open the glass door, he stopped, looking around at the bustling shop. "She did say there were staying busy," he mumbled. Turning to the counter, he grinned at the blonde on the other side. "You must be Hannah."

"Yeah, who are you?" The girl glared at him, glancing down at his bags. "We don't take drop-offs."

He laughed. "That's pretty funny, Hannah. Where's Merideth?" When she only stared at him, he added. "I'm Rider, but I didn't tell them I was coming. It's a surprise. Are they here?"

"They're in the basement." She indicated the back with her thumb. "I guess you can go down there."

"Of course, I can, I'm a guest of Blake and Sarah's," he scoffed. Dropping his suitcase in the office on his way by, he took the painting with him, in case he wanted to present it to her. Below, he could hear his friends' voices wafting up to him. Pausing at the doorway, Rider wanted to watch them for a moment before he interrupted.

"I think they look great," Sarah said, indicating the shelf of old texts.

"Are you sure those aren't Morcant's?" Karen asked, squinting at them doubtfully.

"Quite sure," Blake mocked her, prepared to exchange a bit of banter. Catching movement at the entrance, he dropped the subject. "Hey, Meri, why don't you run up stairs and see how things are going with Hannah?"

"Me? Why should I do it?" she argued, pivoting to see Rider for the first time. "Shit." Three steps each and they flung themselves together. Lifting her, Rider spun her into a happy little twirl.

"Oh my God, I missed you, Boo!" Rider wept, unable to keep his emotions in check.

"What are you doing here?" She panted, her excitement evident. "You should have let me know you were coming!"

"Why? That would have spoiled the surprise." He grinned at her, releasing her enough to stand on her own but not totally letting go.

"I knew you'd come," Blake informed him through a wide grin. Strolling over, he offered his hand. "How was the trip?"

"Fast," Rider exclaimed. "I was sitting alone drinking a beer yesterday when I suddenly realized I needed to be here." He glanced at Meri. "Our stuff will be here in a few days, Boo."

"Our stuff?" Her forehead crinkled at the realization they wouldn't be driving it up themselves. "I thought we were renting a U-Haul."

"No, I got us a moving company. It was simpler. Although we'll need some storage once it gets here," he added, turning to Blake. "We can rent one if you don't have room for it all."

"Yeah, I'm thinking you will rent one," Sarah interjected. Crossing her arms, she studied him. "You seem different."

"I guess that I am different," he confessed. "When I said they are bringing our stuff, I meant all of our stuff. And I canceled the rental on our flat. I told our realtor to sell it ASAP."

"You're moving here permanently?" Joseline asked, her eyes wide with surprise.

"Umm, yeah." Rider pulled Meri around in front of him, staring down at her. "I don't want to lose my girl. Or my new friends. And I'm going to be the best damn enforcer this coven has ever had."

"Well, since I was the enforcer before you, I doubt that," Blake teased. "We just put all my old spell books on the shelf. Have a look and we'll see how you do."

"Seriously? You're going to share your craft with me?" Rider swallowed. "I was a real asshole. I don't know what to say. Or how to thank you."

"Just don't let anything happen to our girls, and that will be thanks enough." Noticing the canvas covered painting, Blake changed the subject. "What's this?" he asked, indicating the parcel.

"Oh, that." Rider picked it up, laying it on the table and unzipping the bag. "This is a little something I started working on after my girl left me." Pulling it out, he placed it gently on the flat surface, using the canvas carrier to cushion it. "I call it the Pretty Lady."

"Wow. She is a pretty lady," Joseline agreed. "Is that me?"

"No, silly! It's me," Merideth announced, tears on her face. "Oh, Rider, it's beautiful."

"You painted that?" Blake stared at it, truly amazed at his

friend's talent. "When you said you were an artist, I had no idea."

"I usually do landscapes and buildings, but this I had to have. Still want me to be your enforcer?"

"Yeah." Blake laughed. "But I certainly think you will need a new studio."

Meri's fingers trembled as she reached to touch the cheeks that matched her own. A tear spilling over, she swiped it away. "Thank you, Boo. I love it."

"I love you more," he countered. "This is what kept me sane after you left. I was so lost without you, I had to have it so I could talk to you."

"You silly man." She pulled him down into a hug. "I'm glad you're here. Did you ride your bike or will they have it on the truck as well?"

"Uh, I sold it," he informed her quietly. "I want to buy a normal car. Maybe one like the rental we had since we both liked so much."

Meri held her breath, afraid he was going to push her to decide on his proposal, but he didn't. Stopping there, he dropped a gentle kiss on her lips, then backed away.

"Let me go have a look at my new toolbox," he exclaimed, pulling one of the books off the shelf and taking a seat to go through it.

## TWELVE

## A Little Flame

AFTER THE OTHERS had gone upstairs, Blake stood, arms crossed as he watched Rider pouring over his tomes. He had had them so long that he knew them all nearly word for word. When Rider pulled out his phone to use the translator, he scowled. "Eventually, you'll have to learn to read Gaelic."

"Yeah, but not today." Rider ran his fingers down the page, searching for familiar words and phrases. Looking up after a few minutes, he noted that the magister still hovered, rubbing his chin and staring at him. Glancing around the room, he sighed. "You should move the coffee pot down here." He put his head down, then mumbled, "Hell, move the whole office down here. It would give you more room upstairs."

Blake snapped his fingers, grinning ear to ear. "Rider, you're a genius!" Turning, he exited to go have a look at the wall between the office and the sales floor. When he reached the top step, he paused to listen to the noise of the customers. Through the doorway, he could see both Karen and Meri moving around and reorganizing the places shoppers had left untidy shelves and displays. At the register, Hannah dutifully rang up purchases and accepted payments. Not seeing Sarah or Joseline, he ventured closer to the opening, then spotted them, both were helping customers.

His happy mood confirmed, he darted into the office to take some measurements. Spying the pot of coffee, he poured a mug full and sat it on the desk. Then he paced the room, counting steps to get a rough estimate of the floor space it would provide, jotting down a few notes as he worked.

Once he had the office lined out, he went around the wall that connected it to the sales floor. He frowned at the loaded bookcase that occupied the other side. He had gone over the reports a few days before, and he knew they didn't sell many of the tomes. Most of their money came from the candles and trinkets. "And soon, the edibles," he said to himself, sold on the idea at last.

Ready to go down and chat with Rider some more, Blake stopped in for a cup of coffee for himself and retrieved the one he had previously poured for his new enforcer, which was now lukewarm at best. Taking the stairs gently, he arrived with both cups still full and placed them on the table, careful to keep the hot one for himself.

Pulling out a chair across from his friend, he declared, "That office idea is perfect. We'll get started moving all of that down here this weekend. We'll put the desk and files in the alcove across the hall and build a wall to close it in like a proper office. The refreshments will come in here, leaving a nice space for the coffee bar and even a few tables."

Deep in his thoughts, Rider didn't respond, so Blake gave him a nudge. "I brought you some coffee."

"Thanks." Rider lifted the mug without taking his eyes off the passage that had engrossed him. He took a noisy sip, then sputtered. "Wow, that's cold."

"Is it?" Blake slurped a swallow from his own. "If we had a microwave, you could warm it up."

"You brought me cold coffee on purpose, didn't you," Rider accused, cutting his eyes up to glare at the other man's smug features. "Are you testing me?"

"Oh, I might be," Blake confessed, leaning back in his chair, and crossing his arms.

"It's not going to work. Nothing could spoil my mood right now."

"I wasn't testing your sincerity." Blake chuckled. "I wanted to see if you would use magic to warm it."

Rider dropped his phone on the table and sat up straight. "How'd you know about that?" Staring at him, he waited, but Blake only grinned. "Are you some kind of witch whisperer? You did the same thing when we first got here. You knew Merideth was a seer after like five minutes of talking to her."

"Witch whisperer," Blake repeated. "I like the sound of that." Standing, he went upstairs and plucked one of the candles off the display, along with one of the little metal pans to sit it in. When he got back, Rider was sipping his coffee. "Did you heat it?"

"No, I took yours." Rider grinned behind his mug, then snickered. "Yes, I used a little warming trick I learned when I was a kid. When I still thought magic was cool and wanted to be like my old man."

"Can you make fire?" Blake asked, taking his seat and positioning the candle on the flat surface between them.

"Which lesson do you want me to do today? Because I was already in the middle of something," Rider groused, indicating his translating. "These spells are pretty dark, by the way. Lots of curses." He thought of Sarah putting one on Lacy and turning her into Caly. "You never actually used any of these, did you?"

"Many times," Blake boasted, then snapped his fingers and ignited the wick.

"Holy, shit!" Rider yelped in surprise. Closing the book, his magister had his full attention.

"Can you do it?"

"I have no idea. I've never tried."

"See if you can put it out."

Rider raised his arm to pinch the flame with his fingers.

Blake held up his hand. "Without touching it."

Rider blew with puckered lips, causing the flame to dance a moment before it disappeared.

Blake glared at him through the curl of smoke. "That's not what I meant."

"I know, but it was too easy to get you."

Rider laughed heartily, and Blake joined him for a small chuckle before schooling his features back to a serious expression.

"Ok," Blake said forcefully. "Light it then, like I did."

Rider gave his fingers a pop, but nothing happened. Trying a few more times, he sighed. "Look, this was fun for about a minute but I'm going back to my reading now."

Blake shook his head slowly. "You give up too easy. Is that why you wanted to be non-practicing? Because it was hard?"

"Nope. I wanted to piss off my old man, and denying the craft totally did the trick. I denounced when I was about fifteen and I haven't used magic on purpose since. Until today." He raised his cup, indicating his warmed brew.

"Yeah, that's a long time to deny yourself. You never cheated? Even a little bit?"

"Not even a little bit. And there were lots of times it would have been pretty convenient. But once I made that pledge to myself, I did my best to keep it," Rider explained.

"Then you are going to need some practice because you, my friend, are an elemental. You should be able to light and extinguish that candle at will, just as I did." Blake snapped again, returning the tiny flame to its place.

This time Rider stared at it, his thoughts turning. "How close do you have to be to do that?"

"Me? Pfft, pretty close. It took me ages to learn to do that. I'm not an elemental so I had to start from scratch. I really am that thing you said—a witch whisperer—but don't tell the girls. It might freak them out or something."

"I doubt that. All of them adore you. Even Merideth thinks the world of you." Rider passed his hand over the candle, letting it singe his fingertips. "I used to do this when I was a kid. I could hold it in my hand if I were focused enough."

"That's good." Blake nodded thoughtfully. "With practice, the skill will return, and much more. What difference does distance make?"

"Someone burned down my studio. The police are looking for an arsonist who lit a fire by conventional means. If they used the craft, they may never be found."

"I'd say they will likely never be caught then. Sorry man." Blake relaxed back into his chair, slurping a few sips. "Have you ever tried water? Or air? Most elementals are limited to one or two, but some can manipulate them all."

"Uh, no. But if I'm going to be practicing, I can give them a try if you want." Rider stared at the little flame, his features drawn as he focused upon it.

"Let go," Blake commanded. "Some magic is better when it's a gentle push rather than a hard shove."

Inhaling deeply, Rider blew the air out slowly to calm himself. A moment later, the flame flickered, then waved around wildly before returning to its previous tranquil state.

"That's pretty good," Blake praised. "You want some matches until you get the hang of it."

"Maybe." Rider grinned. "Don't tell Meri, ok? I want to surprise her with this. My first real magic in over a decade."

"No problem. We'll be closing up shop in about an hour."

"Thanks. I'm going to pick out a few of these to take home, if that's all right." He indicated the tomes remaining on the shelves.

"They're yours now, Rider. You're our first line of defense." Blake stopped at the door to face him. "And it's good to have you back."

"What the hell?" Karen sidled over to Meri, who seemed to be having some kind of silent tantrum. "Are you ok?"

"I'm anxious!" the woman confessed, shaking her hands to relieve her jitters.

"Why? Because Rider is here? You knew he was coming." Karen laughed at her silliness.

"Yes, but you don't understand. He sold his motorcycle. He sold his *house*." Unable to breathe, Meri's eyes grew wide. "I'm in real trouble here, Karen."

Crinkling her nose, the younger girl studied her. "Sorry, I don't get it. You were moving here to Boston, so wasn't he supposed to do those things?"

"Well, yes—" Meri straightened herself, hoping for calm, "but he was dragging his feet. I didn't think he would really come. And I know what this means. He's going to propose again!" Speaking the words made her feel faint, and she flopped her hands back and forth, waving to fan herself.

"Again? He already asked you?" Karen shook her dark locks as Joseline joined them. "Did you hear that, Josee? Meri and Rider are engaged."

"No, we're not!" Merideth snapped, looking around anxiously. "I said he asked me. I didn't accept."

"You didn't?" Joseline gasped. "Why not? That man is crazy about you."

"I know, but it was when and how that got me. Sitting in a rental car in front of his father's house. It was before we came to find you. He didn't even have a ring," Meri explained, wringing her hands once again. "But I put him off. Told him he had to wait. Oh!" she exclaimed. "I told him he had to make it a real proposal. A good one, or something like that."

"Uh oh." Joseline cut her eyes over at her girlfriend. "So now you think he's up to something big."

"I don't know," Meri whined.

"But you do want to marry him, right?" Karen asked, still confused at the issue.

"I don't know," Meri bit forcefully. "I mean I love him, but if I marry him, then he's going to want kids."

"Who wants kids?" Sarah demanded, catching her last words and stopping to join them.

"If Rider and I get married, he's going to want a family," Meri explained, her lip quivering.

"And you don't want that," Joseline concluded, her arms crossing her chest in a judgmental fashion.

"No. I don't think so." Meri sighed, looking at her tall, slender friend with tears in her eyes. "Don't get me wrong, I think it's great, you and Blake and your little bun in the oven. But I have plans. Big dreams, if you will. And do you have any idea what carrying a child does to your body?" She reached for Sarah's hand, grasping it firmly as she inspected her thin frame. "You will never be the same. Having a child is a sacrifice I'm just not willing to make."

"Oh, Meri. You should tell him that. I bet he would understand," Karen consoled.

"Forget him, what do you mean by sacrifice?" Sarah asked hotly.

"She's talking about the punishment a woman's body endures when they carry and deliver a child," Joseline snapped. "It's not fair, really. Men undergo nothing so intrusive. So permanent."

Pulling her hand away, Sarah glared at Merideth. "Thanks. As if I didn't have enough to worry about."

"Oh, honey, I'm sorry." Merideth reached for her, and Sarah reluctantly accepted the hug, rolling her eyes over her shoulder.

"I think you're getting ahead of yourself," Karen concluded. "And we need to get back to work. If we don't stay on top of this place, it will take us hours after we close to get it back in shape."

Meri sniffed, regret pooling in her eyes. She squeezed the soon-to-be new mother and whispered in her ear, "Don't mind me, love. I'm neurotic, and your baby is going to be wonderful. You and Blake are going to be happier than you have ever been," she promised.

"I hope so," Sarah agreed, unable to get her mind off the images of motherhood she hadn't really thought about before she dove in.

## THIRTEEN

# A Gentle Push

Arriving at the Korrigan mansion, Blake led the way into the house, where his coven scattered. Karen and Sarah headed into the kitchen to start dinner, while Merideth and Rider carried his belongings to their room. Pausing in the living area, Joseline caught his eye, emitting a small sigh when he stayed behind as well.

"You seem concerned," he observed once they were alone.

"I am," she confessed, hugging herself. "I've had a bad feeling all day." She stared at the entrance to the kitchen, prepared to end the conversation abruptly should either of the younger women appear.

"Yeah." He exhaled noisily, catching the back of his neck with his hand. Giving it a squeeze, he let the appendage hang there. "I'm glad Rider has rejoined us. It means we can move on to other things." He stared at the lump in her blouse where her cursed pendant hid beneath the cloth.

Unconsciously, she placed her hand over it, then realized what she had done. Her smile relaxed, she offered, "I'd agree with you, but I feel like his being here has only put Meri under a strain."

"How so?" His brow furrowed at the indication of trouble.

"Apparently, my brother wants to marry my sister." Joseline laughed at the dark twist in that statement.

"And that's a problem?" Blake brought down his arm to cross it over the other, covering his broad chest.

"It's complicated," Joseline concluded. "I think you need to talk to them."

"Great, I'll add it to the list." Blake dropped the subject and sauntered into the kitchen to find out about dinner, the girl close behind.

A short time later, Merideth appeared. "Well, that was quick," Blake teased from his chair at the table.

"What was?" Meri took a seat as well, leaving an empty chair between them. Several glasses had been placed in the center, and she used one to pour herself a serving of the wine he had been enjoying.

"Well, it wouldn't really be make-up sex. I missed you sex, maybe?" He sipped his beverage, eyeing her coyly.

"Oh." She flushed, averting her gaze. "No, not yet. Maybe later." She looked up, smiling playfully. "Right now, he's too involved with those books you gave him."

"Ah, he's studying, then. You can take him a plate later if he's too busy to join us," Blake assured. He glanced at Joseline, seeing the deep stiches in her forehead. "Actually, on second thought, I believe I'll have a visit with my enforcer while you lot handle the women's work."

Sarah cut him a cold stare. "That was uncalled for. You may go without tonight."

"You know I'm teasing, love muffin," he countered over his shoulder. Crossing the living area and cutting down the far wall, he arrived at the tunnel that led to the apartments. Not bothering to knock, he opened the door and stepped inside the first one.

Eyes wide, Rider looked up from his flame. "Don't you know how to knock?"

"Yes, but the look on your face was worth it." Blake smirked at him, swirling the glass he had brought with him.

"Where's mine?" Rider asked, perturbed by his perceived failure as an elemental.

"In the kitchen," Blake quipped. "How's it going?" He indicated the candle with a stiff pinky as he slid into the second chair.

"Terrible. I'm getting nowhere." His eyes flicked over to the wardrobe. The small white box he had hidden on top of it could be seen from that vantage point. "Damn," he muttered. Standing, he walked over with his chair. Placing it firmly in front of the cabinet, he stood in the seat and pushed the package further back. Stepping down, he returned to the table and inspected his work.

"What are you hiding?" Blake rocked his jaw, suspecting the trinket based on Joseline's observation when they arrived home.

"It's a surprise," Rider bit curtly, returning to his tapered wax. Blowing noisily to increase his focus, he snapped, to no avail.

"You may think so, but Meri is in a tizzy over that little box," Blake informed him flatly.

Rider's eyes snapped to meet the cool blue ones across from him. "Who says?"

"I'm the magister. I hear things." He paused, giving the other man some room.

"I bet." Rider swallowed, his confidence shattered. "She's going to say no, isn't she?"

"I'm not a seer, Rider." Blake chuckled. "I don't know what she's going to do. But I do know she's scared, and with good reason. Marrying you would be a big step. She gives up a lot of who she is, tying her dreams to yours."

"I would never hurt her," Rider whispered. "What should I do?"

"I can't tell you that either." Blake finished off the glass. "Just know that I've got your back. We're surrounded by women, and that means we have to look out for each other."

"Are you going to marry Sarah?"

Blake shrugged. "Maybe. We are consummated, and our child connects us even further. I'm not sure an actual wedding would enhance what we have. It might even unsettle it."

Rider studied him. Absently, he raised his hand to produce a loud pop, and the wick sprang to life. "Oh my gosh, I did it!"

"See? A gentle push." Blake stood, stepping over to the door. "Blow it out and join us for dinner. Forget about that little box for a few days and let things settle before you put any pressure on her."

"I'm glad the girls came over for dinner," Merideth chattered. She had talked non-stop since they returned to their room. Turning down the blankets on their bed, she smoothed them. Then she inspected herself in the full-length mirrored door of the wardrobe. "I think they make a cute couple."

"Uh huh," Rider coaxed, letting her ramble. Down to his boxers and socks, he placed his candle on the table. After Blake had left him, he had succeeded in lighting it at least a dozen times. This time, he applied a match, then turned the tray, watching the flame intently.

"They've been staying at Joseline's. I've tried to see what's going to happen between them, but I can't quite reach it." She held up her tiny crystal as she pranced around the room, causing her nightie to waft around her legs. She reveled in the feel of it against her bare skin. When he didn't seem to notice, she stared into the ball as she flopped into one of the empty seats.

Sliding into the other one, Rider observed the curve of her breasts beneath the silk nightgown. Pulling himself back to the task at hand, he stared at the flame, watching it dance.

"I really hope they make it," she added, adjusting her crystal again.

"They'll be fine," Rider mumbled, suspecting she wasn't looking for the girls at all. It troubled him that Blake knew about the ring, and where he had hidden it. "They're kismet, remember?" Giving her space was hard, but he was doing his best.

She grimaced, dropping her hands and the trinket into her lap. "What are you doing?" she demanded, ready to change the subject.

He grinned deviously, pinching out the wick. "I've learned something. Or rediscovered it, perhaps." Ready to reveal his secret, he scooted it closer to the center, then snapped the fire back into life.

"Oh, wow!" She sat up in her chair. "Blake taught you that?"

"More or less. I already knew a bit about it. He says I'm an elemental and I can manipulate the flame. Now I just have to learn how to control it. And to extinguish it."

"That's easy."

She leaned forward and he let her blow it out, her giggles music to his ears. "I did the same thing to him," Rider teased. "It was funnier when I did it," he added smugly.

"Oh. I didn't realize it was a contest." Her features drooped and her lip quivered.

"Oh, Boo. I'm sorry!" He snapped the flame back into place. "Do it again."

Her lip sticking out in a small pout, she cut her eyes up at him. "I don't want to. And stop treating me like a child." She sniffled. "If you can't just blow it out, what are you wanting to do with it?"

"I don't know." He shrugged with one shoulder. "I want to extinguish it. To control it with magic. If I can't do that, it's no good to me."

"I don't know if you can control fire," she replied, dabbing at the corners of her eyes. "It's like trying to control a living thing. You can't really force it." She was not really thinking about his little game, and confusion clouded her mind at his callous demeanor.

He leaned back slowly, studying her. "It's a living thing," he repeated airily. "Sometimes a gentle push works better than a hard shove."

"Well, I guess you could put it that way," she agreed, unsure if he was actually talking about the fire.

"I didn't put it that way. Blake did, when he was explaining how to use magic to light the candle." He leaned forward, his excitement growing. "What if I treat it like a living thing. Like we are cooperating with each other, rather than me forcing it." He spread his fingers, waving them gently over the rising heat. The fire followed his movement, and he lifted it away from the wick. Turning his hand, it sat in his palm, hovering above his skin.

"Oh, Boo," Merideth moaned. "How are you doing that?"

"It was your idea," he praised. "I'm not controlling it. I'm giving it what it needs, feeding it with a bit of magic in place of the wick. Kind of leading it where I want it to go, but gently." He closed the palm and the flame disappeared. "Oh my God, it works!"

"So, now you're like a human flame thrower?" Her nose scrunched, she studied him. "It's like I don't know you at all anymore."

"You wanted this, remember?" he spat back. "It was your idea to come here and join the coven. I told you it was a dark world, but you had to see for yourself." She fidgeted in her seat, and he pushed on. "Why don't you tell me what you're really looking for in that little crystal ball of yours?"

"I was looking at the girls," she stammered, obviously lying. Avoiding his gaze, she stared at the floor. When he said nothing else, she swallowed, then said meekly, "I don't want to fight with you, Boo. Let's go to bed and get some rest." She indicated the sheets she had prepared for them with an open palm.

"I'm not the least bit sleepy."

She lifted her chin, gazing at him. "We've been apart over a week. Are you in the mood for a little love making?" She cocked her head, sliding one of the straps off her shoulder and exposing more of her curves.

His lips pursed and his eyes narrowed. "Now we're talking." He pushed the chair back, his boxers like a tent in his lap with his rod holding them up. He nimbly split the opening, stroking himself. "How do you want to do this?" He bobbed his head, indicating the mattress.

The knee-length gown flowed around her as she stood, rounding the table. She raised it enough to straddle him, revealing her lack of panties. She hadn't intended to get any sleep, either. Claiming his lap, she pushed his hand away. "That's mine," she growled, biting his lip gently before she kissed him, taking him inside her and undulating her hips.

Rider's gut twisted. He loved it when she took control. "As you wish." He panted, her bouncing up and down driving him quickly to the point of no return. "But you better slow down, though. Your ride will be over quick."

She stopped instantly, hovering over his stiff shaft. Her heart fluttered, her vision cleared. "Oh, Boo," she groaned. Sinking slowly, she took him inside her. "Don't go too fast."

"A gentle push," he whispered back, faintly aware they were no longer talking about sex.

## FOURTEEN

## Josee's Secret

BLAKE LAY IN NEAR DARKNESS, his arm draped over Sarah's slender form. Still huffing occasionally, she had cried herself to sleep. Pushing up onto an elbow, he studied her profile, his thoughts lingering over what she had told him once they retired to the privacy of their room.

The day had been chaotic, with the return of their enforcer, and Joseline's warning that trouble brewed below the surface. He thought he had headed it off via a quiet conversation with the other man, but as Sarah had angrily informed him, Merideth had been the root of her chagrin.

Unable to doze off, Blake eventually sat up and gently climbed off the pliable surface, being careful not to disturb her rest. Scooping his phone off the dresser, he opened the door and lingered in the hall so that he could talk and still watch her sleep. Noting the time, he scrolled through his contacts. Selecting Ezamay Monroe, he made the call.

"Hello?" she rasped on the other end.

"Hi. I know it's late. Did I wake you?"

"At this hour?" He knew damn well that he had. "It must be important."

"Extremely. We need to make some plans. The quiet kind the rest of the coven doesn't know about until they must," he explained, closing the door to a crack.

"Give me a moment."

"Take your time," he allowed, pacing as he waited. He and Sarah had not made love that night and his thoughts returned to her words. He knew he should inform May, but Meri was her daughter, so he wasn't sure what outcome the sharing would bring.

"Ok, I'm where I can talk."

Her voice stronger, Blake nodded. "Well, we have several things to discuss, and I'm not sure how you are going to take some of them."

"Start with that then," she commanded. "Might as well get the bad news out of the way."

"Ok, Meri told Sarah that having the baby would destroy her body," he stated flatly and waited for her reaction.

"Oh, she didn't." Ezamay sighed. "I'm sorry, Judoc. My daughter has strong feelings about having children."

"She doesn't want any. She shared that tidbit of news as well, which I'm fine with. But Sarah is very fragile right now..." His voice trailed away, and silence filled the air around him. Peeking through the crack, he could see she hadn't moved. "I don't expect you to do anything about it. Merideth is a grown woman. And Sarah is as well, for that matter. I just thought you should know."

"Thank you. And if it's any consolation, I'm sure she didn't mean any harm. She has told me numerous times I won't ever have any grandchildren, so her relationship with Rider will likely end at some point," she finished quietly.

"I also have my doubts, but that is for them to work out." He ran his fingers through his hair, ready to push on. "We also need to talk about Joseline."

"Carry on, then. Is she also upsetting your girlfriend?"

"No, I think our group is getting to her. Or perhaps it's my brother's cursed pendant. Either way, she is definitely carrying a burden. I thought she would finally share it with me this evening, but she only spoke of Meri and Rider instead. It is confusing, really. I'm not sure she fully trusts me."

"I doubt that she fully trusts anyone," May agreed. "Even Karen is probably only let in so far. My oldest daughter has been hurt. Some of that is my fault, and I will gladly take the blame. The question is, what can we do about it?"

"I did find a spell we could use to destroy the amulet, but it will come at a price," he mused, his voice picking up a hint of hope. "If we can work out where and how to perform the ritual."

"You can just come here, as we did last time," Ezamay suggested. "The kitchen was perfect."

"Well, I'm not sure we can leave the store again, even with Hannah here to run things. Someone has been in the store. When we cleaned out the basement, some of Morcant's personal library had been removed. Recently." He waited for her evaluation. When she said nothing, he asked, "You don't think that means something?"

"I'm sorry, I heard a noise and needed to look in on Garrett. You said someone broke in and stole your brother's library?"

"No." He scowled. "I mean, yes someone had been there, and they removed a few of the old tomes, but it didn't look like a robbery. They knew what they were taking, and there was no indication of a forced entry. I'm sure it was someone retrieving them for him." He clenched his free fist, steeling his resolve. "How's Garrett doing, May?"

"Oh, you know. He's carrying the curse like a trooper."

"He's sick, isn't he."

"He won't live much longer," she confessed quietly. "If Merideth wishes to see her father, you should bring the group here and we can perform the ritual."

"I'll think on it. If there's a way we could close the shop for a week, we might be able to swing it. But again, I don't know about leaving it unprotected for that long." He sighed loudly. "Dammit. I was hoping he would fair better."

"He never intended to fight the curse, Judoc. He only wished to save me. I think he has given up on ever being rid of it."

"I should have focused on that. The pendant could have waited."

"No, I think you made the right choice. We need to free Josee as well. Bring her to me as soon as you can and perhaps there will still be time to save both of them."

Blake shook his head, his mind already seeing the end, one he would do anything to avoid. "Thanks, May. I'll let you know what we are able to arrange." Lowering the device from his ear, Blake ended the call. Pushing open the door, he slipped back inside the darkened room, ready to return to his bed and hopefully have a good night's sleep.

Straddling her girlfriend, Karen ran her fingers lightly over her pale skin. "You could use some color," she teased.

"I don't tan," Joseline tossed back. Lifting her hips, she rolled the other girl off her, then took the top. Leaning over her, she kissed her deeply. "I've grown so fond of you, Karen."

"I know. Providence has brought us together but you seem glum about it, love. I wish you would share with me." Karen pushed at the hair hanging around her. "I can keep a secret if it's private."

"It's very private," Joseline confessed. Sitting up, she moved to the mattress. "I'm very tired. Being around the others wears on me." She toyed with Karen's chin, then caressed her cheek. "I want to trust you with my burden, precious. Honest, I do, but I feel it would only weigh upon you as well."

"Try me," Karen clipped, sitting up beside her.

Joseline grinned. "You are so eager to know. And I adore how much you love me. I'm not sure I have ever been so cared for."

"Yeah." Karen shrugged. "Is that the secret?"

"No." Josee sighed, deciding where to begin. "When I was a little girl, people considered me overly emotional. I seemed to be on a roller coaster, constantly up and down. It was exhausting for me, and for them. Especially my parents."

"The ones who adopted you?"

"Yes. They did their best, but they couldn't help me. I went to therapy, and when I finally figured out what was actually wrong with me, I knew no one could help me."

Her face scrunched, Karen studied her. "I don't get it."

"I read people's emotions. I live people's emotions to be precise."

"And you talk to animals? Wow, you have two talents." Karen sounded impressed. "I still don't even have one."

"You do, you just haven't discovered it yet." Jos smiled at her. "And I don't think they are separate. I think my talking to animals is just an extension of my connection to them. Like my connection to people."

Karen's features darkened. "Does that mean you can tell what people are thinking? Like, when they are lying and stuff?"

"No, it's not that specific. It's like sharing their feelings, especially the strong ones. When someone is angry, I'm angry.

When they are sad, I get so worked up I may cry myself. Just from being close to them. I know how the lady in line at the supermarket is feeling, and she doesn't have to say a word to me."

"How exhausting." Karen gasped, grasping the other girl's plight. "You carry your own burdens, and everyone else's."

"Exactly." Joseline caressed her fingers, entwining them with her own. "Don't do that," she warned sharply.

"Do what?" Karen asked innocently.

"Don't feel sorry for me. I don't need or want your pity."

"Eww, I don't like that. It's like you read my thoughts!"

"I don't, I swear. But you *were* feeling sorry for me."

Karen bit her lip, unsure how to reply. "I wish you could turn it off. Or control it and keep it from wearing on you."

"Yeah, me too. But if there's a way, I don't know of it yet. Maybe some day we will find it. Until then, we need to keep this quiet. Can you keep my secret?"

"Of course, I can!" Karen sang, throwing her arms around her lover and pulling her into a firm hung. Holding her, her thoughts turned. "I get it," she whispered, extracting herself from the embrace. "You're the broken match."

Joseline blinked at her. "My shop?"

"Yes. You named it that. It represents you. You spend hours there every day making your candles. But you do it alone, as if you are hiding from the world. Even the candles themselves are like...prophetic. Each one a small light you send out into the world."

Tears spilled onto Joseline's cheeks. "You do understand."

"Of course, I do." Karen tugged at her again, this time wrapping her firmly and rocking her gently.

Jos folded against her, the warmth of her flesh soothing. Enveloped in her care, she sighed. "I've never told anyone so much."

"Blake doesn't know?" Karen stroked her locks gently.

"Well, he knows. He knew right away about my talent. I don't think you can hide much from that man, as far as the craft goes." She sat up straight. "He's afraid of something, Karen," she hissed.

"Of what?" Her brown eyes wide, she waited with shallow breaths. "Blake is our magister. He shouldn't be afraid of anything we face."

"It has something to do with Sarah, I'm certain. Perhaps their child. He hides it well, mind you. But I get whiffs of raw fear here and there." She shivered. "I want him to be strong. I don't like knowing he has this weakness."

"We are strong as a group," Karen corrected. "He doesn't have to be perfect, or domineering, as Morcant had been."

"But he's hiding from it, whatever it is. By denying it exists, he isn't allowing us to deal with it."

Karen shrugged. "Maybe it's something we can't help him with. Maybe it's something he must face alone. Did you ask him about it?"

Joseline laughed, then calmed herself. "No. If he wanted my counsel, he would ask for it, and I would never presume to force my insight on anyone."

"But no one knows of your gift," Karen countered.

"And so it will remain." Joseline grasped her hand, giving it a squeeze. "You have promised me this."

"Yes, I promise. I won't tell anyone about your ability."

"Good. Now, are we making love again or getting some sleep?"

Karen leaned towards her, kissing her with gentle lips. "Oh, honey, you know I'm always up for making love."

## FIFTEEN

## Playing Not to Lose

BLAKE PULLED his Camaro up in front of Spellbound the following morning. Rider hauled himself out of the passenger seat, leaning it forward and allowing the two girls to climb out of the back. "Aren't you coming?" he asked when his magister failed to move.

"I have some errands I need to take care of this morning." He pointed at the door. "Looks like Hannah's already here."

"And here's Jos and Karen. Ok, boss. We'll run the shop and see you when you get back." Rider slammed the door, then greeted his sister with a wave.

Prancing around the front of the car, Sarah rapped on his window, prompting Blake to lower the glass. "Yes, my love?"

"Don't forget we have a doctor's appointment this afternoon."

"I would never forget that." He grinned up at her, and she leaned her head in to give him a peck on the lips.

Meri giggled at them, then presented herself for affection as well. Rider obliged, their kiss deeper, followed by a caress on the cheek before he let her go. "I'm going to the basement to make the coffee, if Hannah hasn't beaten me to it," Meri breathed, then walked on air towards the entrance of the store.

"I'm counting the till, I guess," Sarah announced, following her inside, with Karen close behind.

Pausing in the doorway, Joseline smiled up at Rider. "You two seem chipper this morning. Even Sarah was in a better mood."

"Yes, I think a bit of sleep did them both good. Merideth has calmed down and was far less hostile this morning, which means Sarah is also in a better place."

"I'm glad." Jos entered through the door he held for her. "I want you to know that I'm rooting for you. I think you will make wonderful husband."

Rider stopped cold, gaping at her. "Is there anyone who doesn't know about Meri's misgivings?"

Joseline shrugged. "Hannah, maybe?"

"Cute." Rider stomped away, perturbed. "I'll be in the basement. Enforcing."

"What's that all about?" Karen asked as his back disappeared.

"Who knows. Men are so moody." Jos chuckled. "I'm going to have some of that coffee and get to work on my candle display. I'll need a count before I head over to the Broken Match for today's processing."

"Is my honey going to be delivering all day?" Hannah asked, obviously listening to their banter.

"Probably. I'm going to take Karen with me to help with the dipping, so you will need to step up your game over here." Joseline grinned at her girlfriend.

"Yay!" Karen bounced happily, clapping her hands. "I love helping with the candles."

"We'll be fine," Hannah assured her, leaving the counter

to sweep the store and ensure it would be ready to open on time.

Blake waited in the car until everyone had made it inside, then he eased out of the parking lot. While making the drive across town, he formulated what he wanted to say, knowing full well he really had no control over the conversation in the end. He was going to see Madame Demore, and visits with her seldom went as planned.

Entering her shop, he inhaled deeply, giving his eyes time to adjust. The familiar scent calmed him, as did the dancing light of the candles that lined the walls.

Seated at her table, Matilda greeted him, as if she had expected him. "Good morning, Judoc."

"Good morning, Madam Demore." He stepped forward, taking an empty seat on the client side. "I guess you knew I was coming?"

She laughed. "I don't know everything, my dear. But my day has started beautifully. I feel well, and I'm ready to read." She indicated her large crystal.

"Uh, I'm not really here for that. I'm really only here to talk."

Her brows raised, she obviously doubted that. "What subject should we discuss?"

"Are you familiar with the term herding cats?" She nodded. "Good, then you have an idea of what running a coven is like." He chortled, shaking his head. "I don't remember my brother working this hard to keep everyone in line."

"Heavy is the head," she agreed with him gently.

"Very heavy." He bobbed his around. "I've had a lot on my mind lately. I'm keeping it to myself, but I think Joseline knows. And eventually, I have to share my plan with the others." He sighed deeply.

"You cannot save them all, Judoc."

His crystal blue orbs snapped to meet hers. "Why'd you say that?"

"I know why you've come." She waved her hand over the glass ball, despite his denial of needing her advice. "Your coven is under attack. It reminds you of the past. A time when your wife and son were taken from you."

He rocked his jaw, pondering her words. "Yes," he hissed. "It does feel like that. Like my brother is once again coming after me. Of course, that's only because he is."

"He hurts you through those you love," she concluded for him, watching the movement in her device. "Some are in great danger, even as we speak."

"I know," he confirmed. Shifting in the seat, he crossed his arms defiantly. "But I refuse to think there isn't a way through this. There has to be a way."

"You know the way," she persisted. "You have seen it." She cut her eyes up to glare at him. "Garrett." She dropped the name calmly, then waited for his response.

Blake pursed his lips, pushing hot air between them. "I know there is a cure for him."

"Joseline?"

"And her. I already found the spell I can use to destroy the pendant," he explained shortly.

"But it must be removed from her, first," she finished for him.

Looking down at his open palms, Blake didn't argue.

"You are so different, Blake Korrigan. Not nearly so headstrong as the man who shared his brother's coven. Cold and distant you were, for many decades, but your heart is thawed. Warmed by love and those you wish to protect. You are a better man these days."

Raising his chin, he studied her. "I've tried to be. I want to be. A good magister tends to his coven. He nurtures those in his care." He smiled. "You called me Blake."

"You have earned a new moniker. Judoc of old is only a remnant of the man who sits before me."

"Then why do I feel so angry about all of this?" He swallowed. "What am I so afraid of?"

"You have always struggled with letting go. You have not had so much to lose in over a century. It is understandable you wish to keep it."

"And I'm caught in this living chess match with Morcant. Only I have no pieces to target while all of mine are exposed."

"Very exposed. You will lose some of them. You should prepare yourself."

"You sound like May. She said I made the right choice. But knowing the price hurts like hell."

"Pain is good. It means you are still alive." She cocked her head to the side.

"But I can't lose this, Matilda. It's far too important," he scolded.

"Then stop playing to not lose and start fighting to win." She bit the words harshly, pointing out the flaw in his plans. "This battle cannot be won on the defensive."

"I won't do it without his permission," he growled.

"Then you must ask, and soon." She left her chair, parting her curtain and disappearing into the back.

Cursing under his breath, Blake stood. Pulling his phone from his pocket, he placed a call. Alone in the room, he paced, admiring the dancing flames, teasing them with his fingers. "Hello?"

"Hello, Blake. Let me find Ezamay for you."

The gravelly voice on the other end startled him. He could hear the lack of energy, the hollowness of his tone. "No, Garrett. I'm actually calling to speak to you."

"Oh?" Heaving breaths floated out of the device. "Then you've heard. My sacrifice was and is sound, son. I have no regrets."

"It is not of regrets that I need to speak to you," Blake confessed quietly. "I understand your choice. I respect it. I only wish your suffering could be kept short."

"Then you accept there is no escaping my fate," Garrett rasped.

"None." Blake blinked rapidly. "But there is a way I can help you. And, in turn, you could help another. Joseline still carries the pendant. I cannot destroy it as long as she wears it." He waited, hoping the other man would make the connections without further explanation. "This is hard for me to say," he finally added.

"It's hard for me to hear, but I accept your proposal. Do not speak of this to any of the others. It will be paramount that they do not know the outcome."

"I kept your secret last time, and Merideth still hasn't fully forgiven me," Blake snapped.

"Then I will tell her. Bring the coven here, and we will do what we must to further your cause." The call ended, as if Garrett's word was final.

Staring at the device, Blake sighed. "You can come out now."

The beads rattled as Madam Demore rejoined him. "Your decision is made?"

"It's made," he huffed, not happy with it one bit. "I need to go. I have work to do before I kill one of my oldest friends."

## SIXTEEN

## Good Things

BLAKE MADE a few stops before returning to the shop. Luckily, the contractor he had trusted to work on their renovations would be available and he could push forward with his plan. First and foremost, he needed to get everyone on board without revealing what he actually intended to do.

Stopped at a red light, he tapped the wheel, mumbling to himself. "I hope to God this works." He knew there would be hell to pay if it didn't; and even if it did, the price would be high.

Pulling into a parking space at Spellbound, he climbed out. Breathing deeply, he practiced his smile, adding a bounce to his step as he entered the glass door. "Looks good in here," he called.

Several customers milled about, one with a pile on the counter as Hannah rang up the sale. He nodded at her approvingly. "Can you handle the front alone for a bit?"

"Sure." She grinned, her golden locks shimmering as she shook them.

"That a girl," he praised. Catching Sarah's eye, he

motioned to her and Merideth, meeting them at the circle of chairs. "Where's Karen and Jos?"

"It's production day," Meri reminded him. "They are over at the Broken Match, replenishing our stock." She extended a flat palm, indicating the sparse display.

"Ah, that can't be helped. We need to have a meeting. I've got some arrangements to make, so I'll be in the office until they arrive. Then we can all head downstairs."

"You're going to call them back?" Sarah asked doubtfully. "We have that appointment anyway." She glared at him, certain he had forgotten.

"Aww, pumpkin, don't trouble yourself. We won't miss seeing your doctor."

She crossed her arms and huffed, "And you're coming, right?"

"Yup. Let me go make those calls. We'll go to the obstetrician and have the meeting after we get back." He glanced at Merideth, who had been fidgeting as they discussed their afternoon. "Are you ok?"

"I'm fine." She tossed her honey brown hair, then cleared her throat. "You two go enjoy your baby time. We can talk about your big news tonight at dinner if we have to."

Blake nodded, wondering how much she knew about his day. She was a seer and could have easily circumvented his protections if she had the desire. "I'll be in the back, then." He glanced between them, then turned to walk away.

The girls exchanged brief pleasantries, then returned to tending to the store until he returned. Catching Meri, he advised, "We'll have to meet tonight. Karen and Joseline are swamped and need to put in a full afternoon. We'll all meet at the house around seven. But I have a favor to ask."

"What is it?" She looked at him with wide eyes, almost afraid of what he wanted.

"Can you and Rider rent a car? It will just be for around town. I hate to keep asking you to take the bus, especially when we are pulled in so many directions," he explained.

"Oh, that." She breathed a sigh of relief. "Sure, I'll be glad to arrange one for us, provided Rider doesn't want to simply go buy one."

"That works as well." He grabbed her shoulders, kissing her on the forehead. "You're a gem. Work that out today if you can," he urged, turning to find his girl and head for the obstetrician.

"Hannah, can you mind the front alone?" Meri asked, approaching the counter.

"Why does everyone keep asking me that?" the other girl whined. "Yes. I've got this. Go do what you need to do." She laughed, hoping to cover her displeased tone.

"We just don't want to overwhelm you," Merideth explained.

"I used to work at a coffee shop. This is easy stuff, girl-friend," Hannah teased.

"All right, then I'll be downstairs if you need anything."

"I'll yell if I do," she promised, turning to the customer waiting at the counter.

Leaving her, Meri bounded down the stairs and into the basement breakroom. "Blake has given us a chore," she announced.

Looking up from his book, Rider smiled. "An easy one, I hope."

"He wants us to go rent a car. Apparently, we are too good for the bus."

He leaned back in his chair. "Bus schedules are nice when you have a routine, but we could sure use the freedom. The payment for my motorcycle hit the bank this morning. I suggest we simply buy one."

She bit her bottom lip, pondering if they should. "That's up to you. It's your money, after all. I haven't had real income in over a year."

"Yeah, and I'll be pretty broke as well with the studio disaster unless the insurance comes through. Let's get something small and economical, shall we?"

Nodding, she waited for him to join her before they made their way up the stairs.

"You may have to close up alone tonight," Meri informed Hannah when they arrived at the door.

"No problem. I'll lock the till in the safe at closing if Sarah and Blake aren't back," the blonde agreed.

"Sounds good." Rider knocked on the counter as he passed by, and a moment later they were on the bus and headed to a used car lot.

"Why this one?" Meri asked when they exited the transport.

He silently pointed to a lime green VW Beetle shining in the front row.

"Oh, how cute! Do you think we can afford it?"

"The window price is right. With any luck, we'll talk him down a few bucks and drive it off the lot."

"I like that plan," Meri agreed as they wandered between the vehicles, trying not to look too interested in making a deal.

"Man, what a day!" Joseline lamented. Pouring herself a glass of wine, she placed the bottle on the table, next to the collection of empty crystal in the center. "I think this coven drinks too much."

Karen giggled. "We do enjoy our libations. Taste this for

me." She offered a spoon of sauce, gently touching it to her lover's lips.

"Oh, that's good," Jos praised. Only inches between them, she placed her hands on the hips before her, massaging them. "I can't believe we're over here again tonight. I need some alone time with you."

"Blake said we're going to have a meeting," Karen reminded her, turning back to the stove.

Not giving up her grip, Joseline pulled herself up behind her to grind against her ass. Her hand still on her waist, she pushed it around and down to her crotch, then cupped the mound where her legs came together. Pressing against it, she cooed in her ear. "Let's visit the bathroom. Rub one out, real quick. Your sauce is delicious."

"Oh my God." Karen laughed but didn't push her away. Catching Josee's left hand, she guided it up to her breast. "You make me so hot, baby."

Taking that as encouragement, Joseline pulled at her shirt to slither under it. Finding the edge of her bra, she teased the nipple to a hard nub through the lace. "I'm gonna cum just fingering you," she whispered.

"That's the idea," Karen agreed. Pulling the elastic waist of her shorts, she held it out. "Want to pet the kitty?"

Jos shoved her right hand in and massaged her folds of flesh, her left catching the wire and lifting the cup over the hardened breast. "I can't wait until we get you that piercing," she purred in her ear. Shoving her digits a little further, the tips made penetration.

Karen groaned, humping against the fingers while absently stirring her pot. "Oh, shit," she grunted a moment later, dropping her spoon and leaving it. She no longer cared that they were in the kitchen and wondered if the table would support them.

"Need any help?" Sarah asked from the doorway.

Joseline froze, one hand knuckles deep, the other squeezing a nipple. "Hey, Sarah. You want to take over the sauce?"

Shaking her head, Sarah could only laugh. "You just couldn't wait, could you."

Guilty, Joseline pulled Karen's shirt down to cover her breast, not bothering to adjust the bra. The other, she withdrew as far as the waistband, still claiming Karen's body as hers. "Can you take over here? Karen and I need a break." She pulled at the other girl, tugging her out of the room.

Karen giggled as they passed her best friend. "We'll be back."

"Take your time." Sarah waved as they went by, then sighed as she located her juice in the fridge, noting the couple had crossed the living area and disappeared into the little room on the other side. Karen had put up with her and Blake's noisy fuck sessions at all hours, the least she could do was allow the girls one of their own.

Blake joined her from the back patio a few minutes later, a pile of steaks on his tray. "Where is everyone?"

"Karen and Joseline are making out in the toilet," she informed him tartly.

"Really." Blake stared at the door, imagining the two girls on the other side. "That's hot." He pinched a bite of meat and tossed it into his mouth. "You think they need any help?"

Sarah sneered at him. "You owe me an ass fucking tonight." She sidled up against him, coaxing the hardness in his crotch with her pubic bone.

"You're going to get it right now if you don't watch it," he growled as she bit at his lip. A loud moan carried across the room to them. "Maybe we can use it when they're done."

"Let's slip into the pantry," she suggested, urging him to follow her.

Forgetting dinner, he closed the door behind them, reaching up to twist the bulb and dowse the light. "I can't fuck your ass this way. You don't want to wait? We could go upstairs."

"Here. Now," she breathed airily, yanking her pants down.

"Ok," he sang, his fingers nimble as they explored her in the darkness. She kept herself shaved smooth, and that made finding her dripping honey hole easy. "Damn, you're sloppy." He lifted his fingers to his lips and tasted them. "Oh yeah, this is going to be easy." Releasing the button on his pants, he jerked them out of the way and freed his cock, then shoved her towards the door. "Grab the handle. Don't let anyone open it."

Grasping the cold metal, she was about to ask what to do if they tried, but it came out as a squeak when he hoisted her hips and shoved himself in on the first try. Pumping against her, the door rattled.

"Let go and push against it," he commanded.

Doing as told, she pressed her palms against smooth paint, reducing the sound as he drove into her. Her insides undulated and she gasped. Hearing voices on the other side of the wood panel, she muttered, "Shit."

"It's fine. Don't push so hard, in case they open it. You'll fall out on the floor if they do." Adjusting his grip, he changed his angle, lifting her up with each slow thrust.

"Oh my God, Blake." Coughing sharp pants, she wanted to cry, her orgasm momentarily blinding her. "That was so quick."

Sliding his arm around her, he cupped her for leverage, still taking her in full thrusts. "Your pussy feels so good, baby," he panted. "I'm going to cum now and then fuck you again tonight." He pounded into her violently, rattling the door loudly, then set her back firmly on her feet.

Righting their clothing, it took them a few minutes to collect themselves. Finally, Blake reached up to reset the light, then plucked a can of baked beans off the shelf. "Found them," he announced as he opened the door and stepped into the room.

Seated at the table, the other four had fixed their plates and were quietly enjoying the meal. Using the can opener, Blake calmly opened one end of the silver container, then inserted a spoon. "Here you go, pumpkin," he said lovingly, placing them in front of Sarah, who smiled up at him.

"So," Rider asked, "Should we add locks to all the closet doors? I mean, in case anyone else gets the urge?"

The group burst into laughter, and Blake flopped into his chair. "You're not falling for the whole baked bean thing?" He flicked the spoon handle as he chuckled along with them.

"No." Rider shook his head as he chortled, then gasped for breath between words. "What makes it even better, the girls were in the bathroom—" he pointed at the cubicle "—when we got in here. It took Merideth and me a minute to figure out where you all were, but the noises gave it away," he finished, holding up his hands as if he had hog-tied a steer.

"Well, next time we'll be quieter," Joseline promised, giving Karen a wink.

"Yes, that's the one thing this group is good at," Blake teased, sliding the can over to have a spoon or two. "Sexy time. We might as well enjoy it."

Sarah laughed aloud. "From now on, we can call it bean time."

"Har. Har." He grinned, happy to see her so relaxed about it, as Merideth looked rather uncomfortable. Deciding to let her off easy, he changed the subject. "In other news, we got a good report on the baby," he announced to the others. "They checked everything and even looked at the little heartbeat with this picture machine."

"Sonogram," Sarah supplied between bites.

"Yeah, that." Blake nodded. "Looks like he's going to be fine."

"You always say he, like you know it's a boy. Or like that's what you really want," Sarah chided.

"I don't care what it is, I love it either way." He blew her a kiss affectionately. "Our family is coming, my sweet. And I'm so glad it's with you."

Sarah flushed, pretending to catch it. "Back at you, babe."

Most of them had finished eating by that point, so Blake got down to business. "I like that little car you picked up. Which reminds me, we never discussed your salary for working at the store."

"We get paid?" Rider feigned shock. "I thought coven members were more like slaves."

"No." Blake laughed, despite the presumed jab. "I'll make sure you both get a good salary. Lord knows you both work hard when you're there."

"We all do," Sarah pointed out. "Does that mean we will all get a check?"

"Yeah." Blake placed his elbows on the table and leaned against his hands. "We all need a little pocket money. But we actually have more important matters to discuss. Like renovations."

"What renovations?" Joseline asked, perking up. "I thought you guys just redid the sales floor and the basement."

"Now it's time to move the office and put in the café," Blake informed them, grinning behind his hands at their delight.

"That's fabulous news!" Karen sang. "I thought you were going to drag your feet on our plans. When do we start?"

"Actually, that's what I was working on this morning. The contractor who helped with the sales floor is going to be over to take measurements tomorrow. We close the doors the day after that. He said to plan for ten days. Maybe only seven, but as many as fourteen. Therefore, I'm giving Hannah two weeks off, and we'll reopen then, knock on wood." He rapped on the table and smiled.

"What's he going to do exactly?" Rider asked, concerned about the timing. "I wasn't serious when I suggested moving the office. I mean I was, but I certainly didn't expect you to up and do it."

"We're moving the office to the alcove in the basement and closing that in. Then removing that bookcase, or probably downsizing and moving it. Then we will open up that wall to convert the current office into a coffee bar with a few tables," Blake explained proudly.

"Oh, honey, that sounds wonderful!" Sarah clasped her hands together as she praised his choices. "I'm so glad you came around."

"Well, it was Rider's idea to use the office. And once I went over the numbers with Joseline, it just made sense to convert. People are into that sort of thing, and we really need the store to turn a profit." He lifted his glass, adding, "A toast. To the good things to come."

"Hear hear," the others chanted, taking sips of their wine.

Sipping her juice, Sarah sighed. "So, if the contractor is going to be tearing up the shop, I understand why you are closing it, but what are we going to do in the meantime? Hang around and watch?"

"That sounds rather boring," Karen agreed.

"Well, I spoke to Ezamay as well. Anyone up for a visit to Virginia?" Blake offered, beaming at his scheme.

Rider stopped in mid-chew, swallowing his bit forcefully. Glaring at their magister, he coughed. "Anything going on in good old VA we should know about?"

Silence fell over the table and all eyes turned to Blake. Leaning back in his chair, his grin slowly faded. "I suspect Meri needs to visit her father," he stated flatly, hoping it would suffice.

"Daddy," Merideth said quietly. "He isn't well, is he." Her chin dimpled, and she added, "You are redoing the store so I can make a trip to see him."

"We're all going," Blake stated firmly, then waggled a finger at her. "I haven't given up on him yet, and you shouldn't either." He cut his eyes over at Rider, daring him to defy him.

"Are we going to try to save him?" Joseline asked quietly, her hand absently toying with her pendant.

Watching her, Blake slowly nodded. "We are going to do everything we can."

## SEVENTEEN

## Fighting to Win

CLIMBING behind the wheel of her car, Joseline slammed the door, then gripped the wheel. Squeezing it, she rested her forehead against it and sobbed.

Sliding in beside her, Karen gasped. "What's the matter, honey?" She ran her hand up Josee's back, caressing her lovingly.

"He lied."

"Who lied? What are you talking about?"

"Blake." She lifted herself and leaned back in the seat. Staring at the ceiling, she whined. "Whatever is going to happen to Meri's father, Blake knows he isn't going to be fine."

"Oh, no!" Karen panted, still twisted in her seat to face her partner. Glancing at the door, she asked, "Do you want me to drive? If we sit here, someone is likely to notice."

"No, I can get us home." Wiping her cheeks, Jos started the car and backed into the street. "I'm sorry, babe. I told you I live what they feel. Usually, he's pretty cold and hard to read, he couldn't hide it."

ght you said you couldn't tell when people were

lying." Karen kept her voice low, still stroking the other woman's hair and arm on occasion.

"I can't. But he's in agony. Blake is hurting something fierce over what's coming. Fear and pain pulsated around him tonight."

"And you were forced to share it with him. I'm so sorry," Karen soothed. "I'm going to commit all my spare time to search for a way to help you. Either to control it or block it out, but somehow, you need relief."

Joseline patted the hand resting on her shoulder. "Thank you for understanding. You have no idea what it means to me having you in my life."

"You bet I do." Karen smiled at her profile, giving her a squeeze. "It means the same to me being with you."

Arriving at their little house, the couple climbed out and greeted Caly at the porch. "Let's bring her in tonight," Joseline suggested, squatting to give her a rub. "And we'll have to decide what to do with her while we're in Virginia."

"Are you sure we should go? I mean if Blake's scared..." her voice trailed away as she opened the door and stepped inside.

"Our magister will always do what's best for our coven," Joseline stated firmly. "We have to go and see it through, no matter the outcome." Lifting the cat, she carried her in with her. "Let's take Caly with us when we visit Mom."

"I'm not sure Sarah will like that, being who she is. She's still one of Morcant's minions."

"Pfft, I could be one of his minions for all we know. I have this damn thing around my neck I can't be more than ten feet away from without having a panic attack." Placing Caly on the tiled kitchen floor, she lifted the bowls to give her fresh water and food. "She says she doesn't like the liver cans you bought."

"Oh. Sorry, Caly," Karen moaned. "I won't get those anymore." Resting her knees on the floor to squat on her heels, she petted her gently. "I think Sarah actually misses her," she observed, then dropped her hands in her lap. "I know what you mean about the pendant. Blake's mother transferred the one Sarah had to me. Like an idiot, I threw it into some bushes when I was running through the forest to get away from them. I thought I was going to suffocate before I found it and got it back around my neck."

Joseline tapped the rock beneath her shirt. "She transferred it?"

"Yeah. We don't know how, though. It was a couple of years ago. Plus, Sarah and I were both unconscious. When I came to, it was done, and I was alone." Her lips curled into a deep frown. "Morcant's spells are no joke. I hope you are wrong about Garrett, but I'm afraid you're not."

"My poor sister," Josee lamented, sitting on the floor beside her and crossing her legs. "She's going to lose her father, and I've never even met mine. My real one, at least. Rider says he's a terrible person, but I'd still like to find out for myself."

"We all see people differently. Don't let Rider make that choice for you," Karen advised.

"I won't." Jos leaned her head over to rest against Karen's. "We're taking Caly with us. I don't want to burden Bert with feeding her every day, and if we are really gone ten days, she can't stay here alone."

"We could board her," Karen suggested.

"Oh, God no." Joseline sat up straight, then got to her feet and offered her hand. "We're not locking her in a cage. She can ride in a kennel to get there, but after that she'll need her freedom, either in the house, or outside."

Accepting the appendage, Karen also stood. "Take her,

then. I don't really see what harm it could do." She cut off the light as she led the way to their bedroom, calling over her shoulder, "Goodnight, Caly." Behind her, two green eyes glowed, watching the couple disappear into the darkness.

"I can't believe you wasted your carry-on on a cat," Rider chided as they walked through the airport together. Caly turned in her crate to look at him, and he scowled. "It creeps me out knowing she was once a girl," he added more quietly.

"Please, let's not have that discussion again," Blake begged, holding up his hand in a stopping motion.

"No, let's not," Joseline agreed. Sticking her finger in one of the square holes, she sighed. "I know, but it's the best I can do."

Rider shook his head, then wandered away in search of a snack to take on the plane.

"Ok, everything is set," Merideth announced as she joined them. "Mother has all the bedrooms made up, so there is room for everyone. She even kept all the candles, so we won't have to hunt for those. And she says the cat can have a box in Josee's room. She's having Alice pick one up with some litter for her this morning."

"Ezamay is a kind woman. I hope Caly appreciates it," Blake observed with a grimace. "Did you speak to your father?"

"Yes. He sounds tired, but he's in good spirits. He seems to think we'll be successful." She shrugged. "Thank you for doing this, Blake. I really appreciate it."

Joseline winced. Leaning towards Karen, she whispered, "I think I'm going to be sick."

Overhearing her, Sarah glanced between them, then

whined, "I know I am." Dashing away, she searched for the sign above the door and held her face as she darted inside.

Karen scrunched her nose. "Morning sickness?"

"Yes. She gets it almost every day, but breakfast usually cures it," Meri supplied. "Some evenings she's puny as well. Poor thing."

"It'll pass," Blake chided. "She's going to be fine."

By the time Sarah returned, they were ready to board the plane. Placing Caly's small crate under the seat in front of her, Joseline smiled down at her. "Did you hear? Ezamay is going to let you stay in our room with us."

"Is she happy to be going?" Meri asked from the seat across the aisle, fascinated that they could communicate.

"Oh yes. Once we get her in the house and out of the cage, it will all be fine," Joseline assured her. "And thank you for the first-class seats. It gives us plenty of room for her."

"It's the only way to fly," Merideth agreed with a laugh. Nestling back in her cushions, she had already ordered her drink and hoped to be asleep in no time.

Hours later, the group pulled up in front of the Monroe residence and climbed out of their typical rented van. Rider had driven, as usual, with Blake riding shotgun. The two men had shared a bit of banter, but their growing friendship was obvious to the girls seated behind them.

"I didn't realize they had gotten so chummy," Karen observed as she claimed her suitcase.

"They are getting along a lot better this time around," Merideth agreed.

"Yeah, Rider seldom shows his ass at all these days." Sarah chortled, lugging her bag inside.

Entering the den, Merideth gasped. "Daddy?" Before her, a decrepit figure stooped before the empty fireplace.

"Hello, sweetheart." He offered his arms, wrapping her

into a hug. "Don't worry about how I look. Morcant can't win as long as we are willing to fight."

"But you're so thin," she breathed, pulling away to inspect him. "Are you sure you're going to be ok?"

"I have every confidence in Blake, and the rest of you. I know you will set things right as rain, as soon as we are able to perform the ritual," he informed her.

"We'll be doing that tomorrow afternoon," Ezamay added, joining them. "We wanted to give you two the evening to share."

A slow frown creased Meri's forehead. "I'm going to settle in, but I'll be back down shortly." Leaving her parents, she quickly took the stairs, searching for their magister.

"What's going on?" she demanded once she had located him.

"What do you mean?" he asked innocently, leaning against a door frame, and giving her his best smile.

"I mean with my father. Mother says you want us to have the evening to share. That would only be necessary if tomorrow might end badly." She pulled her hands to her hips, glaring at him.

His features grew strained. "Meri, go enjoy a few hours with your Dad. None of us really knows what tomorrow will bring, and you should take advantage of the time you have."

"I bet," she spat. Turning on her heel, she marched away, ready to get her answers somewhere else. Spying her sister watching her, she caught her arm and pushed her inside her bedroom, closing the door behind them. "Something's going on."

"You feel that way too, huh?" Joseline shrugged. "I've been concerned that they aren't telling us everything."

"They? To which *they* are you referring? There are a lot of people in this house," Merideth snapped.

"Oh, the older crew. Mom, your dad, and Blake, essentially. They have secret talks without us, you know," Jos informed her quietly. Blinking, she hoped not to reveal too much, lest she expose her secret talent.

"Yes, they do. But do you trust Blake?"

"Oh, of course!" Joseline coughed in surprise. "Don't you? I don't think he would ever do anything to harm one of us. Not intentionally. Not if he could help it," she stammered, unsure of exactly what to say. "I know you're scared, but I don't believe he would ever steer us wrong."

Blinking rapidly, Meri sighed. "Thanks, Sis. And I think you're right. He's been through a lot over the years, and I know he's doing his best to fight off his brother's attacks."

"Yes, you know he is. If we keep fighting, I know we can win." She hugged her near twin. "Go enjoy some time with your father. We'll make sure everyone is settled in and the plan for tomorrow is in place."

"Are you sure? I can help," Merideth offered as she pulled away to leave.

"We got it, hon. You go be with your parents. And give them our love," Jos added, opening the door and shewing her out into the hall.

Merideth stopped by her room, ready to consort with the only resource left to her. Inside, she retrieved her tiny crystal ball from her purse. Perched on the side of her bed, she stared into it. A single image appeared to her time and again over the last few days; her father, as he once was, standing next to a tree. She couldn't remember a time or place the image could have come from. Watching it now, he waved to her, his smile broad. "This has to be the future," she whispered, closing her hand around the crystal.

Slipping the device into her pocket, Meri made her way to the stairs and across the hall, ready to join her parents and relax. If her magic wasn't lying, and she couldn't fathom why it would be, she would have her Daddy back healthy and strong very soon. All she had to do was wait for her coven to break his curse and return him to her as good as he ever was.

## EIGHTEEN

## Special Magic

MERIDETH ENTERED the den to find her parents on the sofa. On their laps, they shared an old photo album. "What are you doing?"

"Revisiting the past," her father croaked. "Come and join us."

"Why are you using this old thing?" She took the space they allowed her between them, accepting the book when it was placed in her legs so all three could see it. "Aren't all of these digitized now?"

"Ah, but these are special. From a time when a picture was something you held in your hand and wasn't shared with the world with the click of a button," her father explained. His hand shook as he traced the line of her face in one of the photos. "My sweet Merideth."

"I always loved that dress," she said quietly, also admiring the image.

Ezamay turned the page. "Oh, wasn't that a wonderful vacation?" She pointed to a beach, where Garrett and Meri frolicked in the waves.

"I had forgotten about that!" The girl squealed. "One of the times Daddy was with us at the bungalow."

"I always tried to make time for you," he stated shortly.

"It wasn't a jab, Daddy. I know how important your job was." She sniffled, the past heavy in her heart. Another page, and another group of days gone by swam before her misty eyes. "I thought we were going to talk."

"We are talking," May pointed out. "We are sharing our history."

"Memory lane," Garrett added.

Merideth pursed her lips. "You're afraid the spell won't cure you." She could feel her parents grow stiff on either side. Raising her chin, she looked at each of them in turn. "You're hiding something," she stated flatly.

With slow, purposed hands, Ezamay closed the portal to the past. "Merideth, you are a seer. What is your vision of what lies before us?"

The softness of her tone troubled Meri. "I don't see anything really." Fighting to get her hand into her pocket, she retrieved her crystal. Holding it up before them, the tiny image of her father waved at her again with a single pass of his hand. "I see you, Daddy," she explained. "You are standing next to a tree in a place I've never seen. And you wave at me."

Garrett curled his hand around hers, holding the ball steady as she stared into it. "I wish I could share your sight."

"Can you see him, Mother?"

"I'm afraid not, my dear. It was always Teddy who had the visions," her mother confessed.

"Teddy." Meri dropped her hands into her lap. "He's the one who gave me this crystal. What if I'm seeing one of his memories? What if this is the past and not really the future?"

"I'm not sure, dear." Ezamay lifted her chin, her lip catching a quiver.

"And now you're crying." Meri sighed loudly, flopping back against the cushions and resting her head against them. "I wish you would just tell me what is going on. You two are obviously up to something."

The couple exchanged a glance across her lap. Taking the book, Ezamay stood, ready to return it to its place on her shelf. "I should let your father explain."

"You'll stay with us, please, darling," Garrett rasped.

"Of course. But this is your decision. And hers," May agreed.

"My dearest child," Garret began, taking her hand in his. "There is no magic that can cure me. Morcant's curse is too strong, and I'm afraid that soon I will be no more."

"What?" Merideth gasped, confusion swimming in her brain. "But that's why we're here. Blake said—"

"Blake would say anything to get you here," her mother countered. "He knows this is one battle we cannot win." Her face drawn, Ezamay took a ragged breath. "Your father suffers greatly these days."

"Unbearable pain," her husband agreed.

"Oh, Daddy," Meri moaned, leaning against his frail chest and weeping. "Please don't say any more. I have to believe the spell will save you."

"You aren't here to save me, pumpkin." Garrett hugged her as tight as he could. "You are here so that I can help you save Joseline."

Meri instantly pulled herself from his grasp. Sitting up straight, she glared at him. "Save Jos! How? *Why?*"

"My precious daughter," he soothed, stroking her arm. "The pendant she wears will slowly drain her. Morcant has cursed her through it, and like me, it is only a matter of time before she will fall to it. And to his will."

"No," Merideth breathed, shaking her head slowly. Tears

had trickled onto her cheeks, a large, single drop of sadness dripping from her chin. "Please, no."

"Meri, listen to us," her mother stated firmly, reclaiming her seat beside her. "This is the most important thing we will ever share with you."

Taking over, Garrett rasped, "This was my choice. I wanted to save your mother, and I have. Now I have the chance to save your sister. That is, if you let me."

"If I let you!" Her voice shrill, Merideth shook her head. "You're putting this on me?"

"It must fall to you," her mother stated firmly. "If you have doubts. If you cannot be a part of the ritual, then we shall not attempt it."

"But be warned," Garrett added with a squeeze of his wrinkled digits. "My end is near, whether we perform the ritual tomorrow or not. All we can do now is shorten my time."

"And end his suffering," Ezamay agreed.

Meri broke into loud sobs, shoving her face into her hands. "I knew it wasn't true. I knew..."

A parent on each side, they enveloped her with their arms and their hearts. "My child," Garrett whispered, "as you are aware, I lived apart from the craft. Never have my lips uttered a curse or a charm. But this is the most special magic one can offer. The light of my soul I freely gave to your mother, and will share with Joseline, if you will let me. Go up to bed. Sleep on the decision and bring fresh eyes and understanding with the dawn."

"I'm not leaving this room," she challenged. Pulling away, she wiped at the tears. "I'm staying here with you. Both of you." She raised her chin, daring them to try and send her away.

"I don't know if three can share this couch," Ezamay teased.

"We'll manage," Meri clipped. Rising, she opened the trunk in the corner and produced the blankets and pillows that were stored there. Swiping her cheeks again before she turned around, she put on a brave face. "Remember the blanket forts when I was a child?" she asked after rejoining them.

"I remember my knees popping when I crawled out!" Garrett laughed. "You were such a joy to raise, my Meri. I missed you so dearly when I was away in Washington."

"And I missed you, as well. I love you so much, Daddy." Unable to stop her trembling limbs, Meri unleashed the flow. Sobbing, she curled into the space between them, pulling the blanket up to her chin. Inhaling deeply through her nose, the scent tore away the years. They held her, letting her cry, until she dropped off to sleep.

"What's all this?" Rider demanded. Standing in the doorway to glare at the trio the following morning, he placed his hands on his hips.

"Shh. Let them rest," Blake chided. "We can set everything up and have it ready when they are."

"But Meri didn't even come to bed last night!" Rider informed him angrily as he followed their magister into the kitchen.

"Yes. Last night was for them to share." Glancing around to see that they were alone, he added, "Please, Rider. Don't make this harder than it is going to be."

Catching his breath, their enforcer stared into Blake's cool blue eyes. "What's going on?"

"I can't tell you that. It's up to Meri, and I don't want the girls catching wind of what is to come until we're ready," he explained briefly.

Looking him up and down, Rider squared his shoulders. "Man to man?"

"Man to man," Blake agreed. "It won't be pretty."

"We aren't here to save him, are we," Rider concluded.

"No. I can't tell you more than that until it's time. Can you help with the candles and the island? Like we did before," Blake suggested.

"Yeah. The boxes are stacked in the closet in our room." Rider blinked at him, struggling to make sense of things. "I'll bring them down and start lining the walls."

"Good. Get the girls to help you. We'll soon know if we're going through with this." Blake clapped him on the arm in affirmation.

"Sure. I'll get right on it," Rider agreed before stomping out of the room.

## NINETEEN

## All on Me

WHEN MERI AWOKE the following morning, she found herself alone on the sofa. The blanket tucked around her, she curled it to her nose, inhaling the intoxicating scent. Through the blinds, she could see bright light and knew the day was in full swing.

Standing, she stretched, forcing her blood to flow. Her eyes burned and her heart ached. She decided to go have a shower, but she knew it could never quench the pain that seared her soul like the sun scorches the desert.

Leaving her sanctuary in the den, she heard voices coming from the kitchen. The laughter drifting on the air seemed foreign. Painful. As if it had no place in her world. Leaving it, she crept up the stairs, hoping to avoid the blissful faces that would only bring her to tears should they meet.

Beneath a cold spray a few minutes later, she leaned against the wall. The cascade tumbling over her, it was all she could do to breathe. Hot tears streamed down her cheeks; she would have thought they had been drained the night before. "Apparently not," she mumbled before succumbing to a fresh wave of sorrow.

Below, Blake stood with the others in the kitchen, a cup of coffee in his hand. "I love what you've done with the place." He offered the brew as a toast to Rider.

"It wasn't just me." The other man laughed. "The girls helped."

"Yes, we did," Joseline added cheerily, sipping her own cup. "And I believe we are all set. As soon as my sleepyhead sister gets in here. Maybe we should light the candles while we wait."

"Oh, hey!" Rider hopped about, placing his coffee on the counter, and holding up his hands. "I'm ready to do this," he announced.

"Ready to do what?" Karen asked, eyeing him warily.

"This." He held up his hands, palms up to focus himself, then closed his eyes. When he opened them, he stared straight ahead. Moving his arms slowly, he ignited the wicks as if a wall of fire had swooped down upon them, circling the room with a slow pivot until every single one burned with a tiny flame.

"Holy shit!" Joseline whispered, breathless. "I didn't know you could do that."

"Actually, I'm a little disturbed by this," Karen added, her eyes darting around to inspect his work. "Aren't any of you bothered by it?"

"It's not that big a deal." Rider chortled. "Blake can do it, too."

"I can to an extent," Blake clarified, raising a stiff digit. "One at a time."

"I think it's sexy," Sarah added, giving her lover a wink. "You can light my fire any time," she cooed, then laughed with the others joining her.

"Wow. So, this is your talent," Karen lamented to Rider, her lip forming a small pout. "A fire starter. Why didn't you tell us?"

"I can put them out, too," Rider bragged. "And even I didn't know until Blake explained it to me. He's the Witch Whisperer—" He caught himself too late. "Oh, damn."

"He's the what?" Sarah asked tartly.

"He's the...witch whisperer," Rider repeated more quietly. "Sorry, man. I blew it."

With a half shrug, Blake sighed. "It would happen eventually. Don't sweat it."

Sarah placed her hands on her hips, facing their magister to give him a squinty glare. "What does that mean exactly?"

"It's my talent. My gift. I read witches. I can even tell when people have been using the craft, even just a little bit," he supplied. "It's not a big deal."

"Oh really," Karen snapped. "So, when are you going to whisper up mine?"

"Hey, I don't give you the talent," Blake teased. "I only take what you have and help you develop it."

"Are you saying my girl has no talent?" Joseline scowled at him.

"No, she has one. When she's ready to develop it, I'll be here," Blake replied, returning to his lukewarm beverage.

"Can you at least give me a hint what it is?" Karen thrust her arms across her chest.

"Nope. Not until you're ready." He grinned at her over the rim of his cup, enjoying the torture.

"Well, the candles were the last step in our preparations," Joseline observed. "How much longer is Meri going to take do you think?" She addressed Rider, as if the woman in question belonged to him and he should know.

"It's fine, we can wait," Sarah interjected. "It will give me a little longer to practice the spell." She pulled her folded yellow sheet from her pocket and wafted it at them, indicating her devotion to the cause.

"About that." Blake stepped over to her, relieving her of the page. "I'm going to be the caster on this one, love."

"What? Why?" Karen sputtered. "Sarah's the best in the coven, or don't you agree, Mr. Whisperer?"

"Oh, I agree," Blake nodded, "but this one is all on me."

"What's that supposed to mean?" Joseline barked. Forgetting their joviality only moments before, she clearly picked up on his undertones of guilt mixed with sorrow.

"It means, no matter what happens, I'll take the blame." He raised his chin towards her, and a silence fell over the group as Merideth crept into their midst.

Her eyes hollow, she avoided looking at any of them directly. Instead, she weaved her way through to select a mug from the cabinet and poured herself a cup of java. Sipping it black, she stared at the wall, her odd behavior putting the rest on edge.

"Hey! We're kind of celebrating in here," Karen called to her, then she closed the distance between them and dropped her arm across her shoulders. "Cheer up, ladybug. Your dad is going to be fine!"

Meri cut her eyes over at her best friend, then pivoted slowly to face the crowd. "I take it you haven't told them?" she calmly asked Blake.

"I was waiting for you," he replied softly. Grasping his cup by the rim, he placed it on the counter and faced his coven. Squaring his shoulders, he cleared his throat before he began. "So, as some of you might have guessed, we've hit a bit of a snag with today's ritual."

"Oh, no," Joseline lamented under her breath, his pain pulsing within her.

"Yeah," he continued, running his fingers around his

mouth. "But before I say anything else, I need your final word." He stared at Merideth, waiting.

"You're going to make me say it?" she asked curtly.

"I have to. We have to be very clear on what's going to happen here today." Blake tapped his foot, the noise a heavy thud in the silence.

Meri cut her eyes over to her father. "I love you, Daddy."

"I love you too, sweetheart." Shuffling around the island, Garrett wrapped her in his tired arms. "That's good enough, Judoc. Tell everyone what's going on and stop tormenting her."

Nodding, Blake inhaled deeply, blowing the breath out in a slow hiss. "What's going on..." he echoed. "My brother is powerful, and his curses are...unbreakable. I've scoured everything in my reach and found no way around this. Garrett is suffering immensely with the one he carries for his beloved Ezamay, and he will continue to do so until we either move the curse to someone else, or he dies from it." His voice broke at the end, and a flurry of gasps and whispers circled the group before they fell silent once more.

Holding her father, Meri spoke up. "We can end his suffering. In the ritual today, we can let him go." She pulled away enough to look into her father's eyes. "That's what I'm going to do. I'm going to give you peace, and I'm going to let you go." Extricating herself from his grasp, she moved to her point on the star. She straightened herself, indicating her readiness to face the task.

Taking her cue, Garrett moved towards the wide table that occupied the center of the room. "Stop being so glum," he rasped. "I'm choosing this. I took Ezamay's curse gladly; and what I do today, I do with equal fervor." He turned, sitting on the edge of the counter, ready to stretch out upon it.

"Not yet," Blake commanded. "Joseline, I need you to give him your pendant."

"My what?" She stared at him with wide eyes.

"Your amulet. The one my brother gave to you. I need you to present it to him." He raised his hand, indicating the motion of handing it over.

Removing it, Josee's fingers trembled. "I don't understand," she whispered. Taking Garrett's outstretched palm, she placed the pendant in the center, then coiled the chain on top of it.

"Has anyone else ever touched this necklace?" Garrett asked.

Meeting his gaze, Jos swallowed. "No. No one. Not since Morcant presented it to me."

"Then I accept this gift from you," he concluded. Closing his fingers around it, he scooted back and stretched across the hard surface. He folded his arms across his chest, the stone directly above his heart.

"Here," Ezamay offered, placing a pillow under his head.

"What exactly are we doing," Joseline demanded, pivoting to face Blake squarely. "Is this what you've been planning? The whole time it was about me?"

Blake's Adam's apple bobbed, but he did not reply. Cutting his eyes over at Meri, he waited.

"Everyone to your places, please," she announced. "You all know your positions. Joseline, love. You take the head, where Garrett stood last time. Mother, please stand at his feet. Sarah, you are on Blake's point, as he will be the caster." Her voice faded by the end, and she blinked rapidly.

Joseline didn't bother hiding her tears. "I can't believe you are doing this," she sputtered. "I want to know...exactly...what is going to happen to him," she panted.

Blake glared at her from the side, his body stiff. "He's

going to die, Joseline. I can transfer the curse to him, but the only way to break the link to you is to destroy the stone, which requires a sacrifice. When he dies, he will take both curses with him." His lips pressed together, forming a stiff line.

Before him, Garrett raised his empty hand, offering it to his friend. Seizing it, Blake squeezed it firmly, and Garrett groaned. "You are a good man, Judoc. Thank you for doing this."

"You shouldn't thank me," Blake whispered, a tear spilling over and staining his cheek. "Not for this."

Her suffering equal to his, Joseline wailed loudly, but she remained in her spot. The fire dancing around them, Rider prompted, "I think you should begin."

Giving the hand a final shake, Blake released it, returning it to the old man's chest and giving it a final pat. Then he raised both of his towards the ceiling. His voice low, he bit the words angrily. Not concerned with the streams that coated his cheeks, he closed his eyes and let them flow, allowing them to fuel his passion.

Standing across from Rider, Merideth bit her bottom lip. Around her, the others were drawn into the chant, and she could hear their voices rise. Refusing to take part in it, she whimpered, noticing that Rider's lips moved in the rhythm of the mantra.

Drawn by the power surrounding her, Meri's body swayed. The flames flickered and a familiar breeze swirled through the room, causing the tiny points of life to dance wildly before returning to their sedate positions. Unable to resist the call of the spell, she whispered the words.

Before them, Garrett grunted, arching his back against the hard surface. "Korrigan!" he screamed. "I'm coming for you, Morcant! What you have brought down upon my house, I will return to you tenfold!"

Merideth sniffed, her cheeks damp. Tightening her jaw, she pushed herself into submission. Her voice raised, she joined the undulating recitation, willing her father's spirit to be free and his torturous pain to be relieved.

Outside, a dark cloud had rolled in the moment Blake began chanting his curse. The wind howled and hail beat against the side of the dwelling, but Morcant's fury could not reach them within the walls fortified by his brother's magic. Lightning split the sky and a loud crash of thunder boomed.

Inside, the electric lights fell dark, leaving them with only the flickering light of candles to watch as the last breath left Garrett's body. Holding his tongue, Blake stared at the man's chest, conflicted by the need to see it rise and confirm his life and knowing that it never would again. Rain fell against the walls of the house, cleansing it as Blake whispered, "Goodbye, my friend."

## TWENTY

## From the Heart

---

MERI'S CHAIR squeaked as she shifted. Seated in the front row, she stared at her father's casket over his open grave. Her eyes dry, they burned when she blinked them. No tears left to cry, she sat waiting for the kind words of the eulogy to end. Her small crystal in her hand, she snuck a peek. Her father still stood next to the tree and gave her a solitary wave.

Beside her to the right, Rider inhaled deeply, letting the breath out slow and easy. Reaching for her hand, he wound his fingers through hers. He wished to comfort her, but the only thought he could conjure was that her father was at peace. He saw little comfort in that, at least for the moment.

On her left, her mother dabbed at her soft blue orbs with a hankie. Her crying soft and low, Ezamay mourned the man she had married. The one she had loved for so many years. The father of her youngest daughter. They had done what they had to do, by his wishes and her agreement, but Ezamay doubted it would ever feel right.

The second row of chairs held the rest of their coven, all sniveling and doing their best not to blubber; and at the very back stood Blake. Wearing a dark suit and shades, he could have passed for a bodyguard out of the latest action thriller. Behind them all, he folded his hands in front of him and watched. The wind catching his wavy hair, it blew in short bursts, chafing his resolve.

The movement of air held a sacred energy. Relaxing into it, Blake became lost in the moment, his mind inspecting each detail of the ritual the week before. From the moment it ended, time had crawled. The days following were spent helping Ezamay with Garrett's final affairs. Only a scant five days, it might as well have been a month.

Walking to the long black car a few minutes later, Blake claimed Ezamay's side. Before they reached it, he leaned in to whisper, "You should return with us to Boston. There is an evil wind here."

"I felt it," she replied calmly, raising her chin, "but your brother will not scare me from my own home."

"Call it a visit then," he pushed, helping her climb inside.

"I'll think on it," she clipped, adjusting herself against the upholstery as the others settled into their seats around her.

When they arrived at the house, each retreated to their rooms where they changed into more comfortable clothes. Reporting to the dining room when they were decent, a special meal had been laid out for them along with a few bottles of wine. Seated at the head of the table, Ezamay's daughters flanked her with their partners at their sides.

Blake took the opposite end, with Sarah to his right, and the empty chair to his left. Staring at this, he placed his elbows on the table and folded his hands to lean on.

Watching him, Ezamay sighed. "Do not regret what is done," she instructed.

Cutting his eyes up to see that she spoke to him, Blake removed his arms from her table and sat up straight. "I will always regret his loss." He selected a fork and made the appearance of eating.

"Then mourn his passing, but do not forget the cause for which he suffered. He loved us dearly," she declared.

"I swear I felt his spirit at the service," Karen announced. "Like his voice whispering on the wind."

Meri stiffened in her chair and stared at the girl across from her. "Those were not my father's words."

Rider dropped his fork, then applied his napkin to his lips. "Can I take it that everyone heard the whispers in the wind?"

"My brother is upset we would make so bold a move," Blake supplied quietly. "I would not trust anything you heard." He held Ezamay's gaze, waiting for her assessment.

Rather than add to his assertions, she sipped her wine and continued the meal. After the pause grew long, Josee asked, "Did you not hear it, Mom?"

"Oh, I heard," she assured. "At the moment, I am contemplating our magister's offer."

"Offer?" Merideth echoed, her thoughts on Joseline's observation about the older group. "Have you been making plans without us again?"

Blake sneered, scooping a few bites before he calmly replied, "Your mother is invited to Boston. She has no ties here I am aware of, and perhaps her children might be enough to persuade her."

"Oh, Mother!" Meri exclaimed.

"Yes!" Joseline declared. "I agree. I have a spare bedroom. You would be perfectly welcome there."

"Why would she stay with you? Your house is so small. And we have the second efficiency apartment she could have all to herself," Merideth argued.

"I'd have to move my clothes," Rider pointed out, drawing everyone's attention. Straightening himself anxiously, he added, "I'm using the closet in that room since the wardrobe in ours is a bit small."

"Your pants are safe, Rider," Ezamay teased. "If I go for a visit, it would only be temporary. No need to displace anyone. As I told Blake, I will have to consider it."

"We can stay on here for a while," Merideth quickly added. "I'm not sure how the renovations are going, but the store is closed until we reopen it." She turned her attention to their boss. "Unless you're afraid someone will break in."

"No, I don't think anyone would. Whatever my brother was after, I'm sure he has already removed." He lifted his glass, taking a few sips before he confessed, "I've already warned Hannah that we will be overdue on our return. I've compensated her, of course, in hopes that she will still be available when we do."

"Good," Karen retorted. "Then it's settled. We'll all stay here until we decide what to do next." Finished with her meal, she dropped her napkin across her plate and sauntered out the door.

"Wow. She seems pissed," Rider observed.

"She's just upset," Joseline explained. "Most decisions are made without our input. Or we have our say after the fact. She doesn't really feel like a partner. You know, in the store. Or the coven."

"I'm putting in her little coffee bar," Blake pointed out curtly, turning up his palms. "That should count for something."

"Oh, Blake." Meri giggled, earning a dark glare.

"Do you think that's cute? Her little tantrum?" Blake ground his teeth. "In case anyone hasn't noticed, this isn't a democracy. Spread the word." Pushing back his chair, he also left the table.

"Wow." Meri fanned herself for a moment. "Tempers are a little short around here today."

"Blake's just worried. And heartbroken, of course," Joseline pointed out.

"What makes you say that?" Rider asked, studying her.

Blinking at him, Jos slowly shook her head. "Well, obviously, of course."

"It's not very obvious to me," Sarah seconded. "First you're explaining what's up with Karen. Then you're telling us how Blake feels. Since when are you such an expert on how everyone else is doing."

Joseline swallowed, laying her fork on the table. Her eyes meeting Meri's, she sighed. "Maybe I'm just a little better at understanding people," she defended.

Ezamay shook her head. "This is why covens are bad. You either have to all mind your own business or you can't keep any secrets because others take it the wrong way."

Not sure how to respond, Joseline turned to her mother, the color draining from her face as she considered kicking her under the table.

"You might as well tell them," the older woman continued. "They're going to figure it out eventually anyway, and you get a few points if you don't make them do all the work for themselves."

"Tell us what?" Meri asked, tired of the games.

Clamping her mouth shut, Joseline reached for her glass. Gulping a few large swallows, she sloshed it as she returned it to the table. "I'm an empath," she blurted.

"An empath," Rider repeated. "Meaning you are empathetic. You understand people's feelings."

"Yes." She cut her eyes over to meet his. "I feel what you feel."

"We've been together for months, and you're just now

telling us this?" Merideth's voice grew loud. "We're family. Siblings. We should have been the first people you told!"

Hearing her, Blake strolled back into the room. "I'll take the blame for that one, too. I told her not to say anything because it would make the rest of you feel awkward around her."

"No one is blaming you, Blake," May soothed. "Why don't you sit down and we'll have dessert."

"Fuck dessert!" he shouted, his arms flailing. "The only thing I want right now, I can't have. And I'm so God dammed pissed about it!" He sank to his knees, sobbing. "I just want to go home and forget we ever came here."

Out of her chair, Sarah rounded the table and dropped down beside him. Pulling him into her arms, she squeezed. "Shh. It's ok, Baby."

"It's not ok," he whined. "I didn't want this. I didn't want *anyone* to get hurt. And Garrett is dead. He is never coming back."

"And that's not on you," she persisted. "That's on your asshole brother. He started this. Look what he did to me!" She pulled an arm away to indicate her altered body. "All we have is each other." She wafted a hand, indicating the group still seated at the table. "This is our family now. Together, we are going to fight him. So don't you give up on us now, Blake Korrigan. We need you. None of us would have wished for what happened, but we all understand it. We accept it. And we are all willing to do whatever it takes to make sure it all ends here."

Sitting back on his haunches, Blake stared at her. "I don't know if we can beat him," he confessed, his face damp with tears. "I was so devastated when he took my son. When he destroyed my Morna. I spent an entire century not caring about anything just to escape it. And now he's doing it. All. Over. Again." He used his fists to emphasize his final angry words, punctuating each with a punch to his thighs.

Catching his chin in her hands, she lifted it, planting a gentle kiss on his lips. "I'm sorry for what happened to them, but we can't dwell on the past. Here, now, this is us. And together, we are going to make the best stand that we can. We will follow wherever you lead. Or we'll vote if you want to share that burden, but we do it together. That's all I can say." Kissing him once more on the forehead, she sat on the floor next to him, waiting for him to decide.

"I'm going to go to Boston with you," Ezamay announced, breaking the silence.

"Oh, did my little fit convince you?" he asked, only half joking. Wiping at the mixture of sweat and tears on his cheeks, he sighed. "Maybe you should run the coven. I think I suck at it."

"No way," the three siblings at the table said in unison. Looking at each other, the trio broke into a small round of giggles.

"You've helped us all, man," Rider pointed out, twisting in his chair so he didn't miss the show. "And it takes a real badass to cry in front of women. You've done that twice now."

"Oh really." Blake chuckled at the observation. "I thought that made me a number one pansy."

"No, sir, it doesn't. You come from the heart. Your brother will never have that. There isn't one of us who doesn't know how much you care about them. If Karen wants to be all salty because you're in charge, let her. In the end, we know you are going to make the best choices for us. Straight from the heart." Rider thumped his chest. "Believe it."

"I have to agree." Meri grinned at her boyfriend's odd display. "I've used my gift every day since I met you, and I'm not ashamed of it. I'll get better at it, and I'll have you to thank."

"Same here." Joseline waved her hand at him as if she were in a Miss America pageant. "We love you, too. Please don't give up on us."

"Pfft," Karen huffed from the doorway. "Easy for all of you to say. His brother already killed me once. And it was his mother who saved me, so before you get all teary eyed, ask him what my talent is."

"Don't even bother." Blake shook his head. "I told you. I'm not sharing until you are ready. Until you have some inkling of what it is. It's dangerous." He stood to face her. "I'm sorry, but I can't budge on that."

Her cheeks read hot, Karen squealed, and the plates on the table vibrated. "I hate you, Blake!" she bellowed, just before her glass shattered. Bits of debris scattered across the setting, the girls screeching as they covered their faces.

"What the hell was that?" Rider shouted, standing slowly. "And what are you grinning about?" He stared at their magister, waiting for his reply.

Blake only shook his head, turning to the girl. "See, that wasn't so hard, was it?"

"But, what happened?" Karen asked, holding out her glass-coated arms. Small beads of blood formed where a few shards had nicked the surface. "I wasn't even touching it." She wafted her hands towards the chair she had recently vacated. "It was still on the table."

Ezamay wiped her face with her napkin, then got to her feet, shaking her head. "Sorry, Blake. This is your circus to run. I'm not fit to be in charge of the young."

"Are you ok, Mother?" Meri asked, seeing a drop of blood on her crinkled cheek. She stood next to her, inspecting her few cuts. "Let's go upstairs and we can doctor our wounds together."

"I think I'll join you." Joseline slipped from her seat, close behind.

"Blake," Karen stated flatly. "Why did my glass explode and why is everyone running from me? You said it was dangerous, but what is it?"

"You should watch your temper," he chided, raising his brow at her. "You don't have to be angry to use it. In fact, you'll have better control when you're calm."

"Is this like my fire thing?" Rider asked, inspecting his exposed skin for cuts. "A gentle push over a hard shove?"

"Something like that." Blake nodded, glancing at Sarah, who had either slipped into deep thought or shock. "Babe, are you with us?"

"Yeah," Sarah said quietly. "She's that spoon bending guy," she added.

"She's what?" Rider snapped.

"The guy. The one who moves things with his brain." Sarah shook her hands, trying to trigger the right word.

"No way. That guy's a fake." Rider laughed, then paused, holding up a sparkly arm. Watching how the bits of glass caught the light, he gasped. "Oh, man, this is big. I think this might even top fire."

"Only if she learns how to use it, my friend," Blake observed, slapping him on the back before grasping Karen by the arm and leading her outside.

## TWENTY-ONE

## Home Again

"I THINK you have the coolest talent ever," Joseline announced as she flopped into one of the chairs in the mansion living room.

On the sofa next to her, Karen sat with a deck of cards. Pulling up one at a time, she telepathically floated them across to form a new stack on the table. "It is pretty neat, huh." She giggled, losing one, which fluttered to the floor. "Damn it." She leaned over to inspect it where it lay. Holding up her hand, it floated up to her, and she grinned. "At least I feel like I'm really part of the coven now."

Carrying a beer in each hand, Blake entered from the kitchen. "God, it's good to be home," he announced as he sank into the chair on the other end of the grouping.

"Two beers?" Sarah observed from his end of the couch.

"I'm having mine and yours," he teased, chugging one of them and placing the empty on the table between them. He took a noisy sip from the other, then grinned at her.

"Thanks. I'm glad it won't go to waste." She rolled her eyes and returned to the conversation about talents. "I have to agree, making shit float is pretty cool. It makes being a good caster seem a tiny bit lame." She used her fingers as a visual on the tiny bit part.

"I still like mine," Merideth clipped, stepping over Karen's legs to take the middle cushion of the sofa.

"Where's Mom?" Joseline asked. "Did you leave her alone upstairs?"

"She wanted to have a shower and maybe a nap. She's pretty happy with the room, though." Meri smiled at Karen. "I hope you don't mind her using it."

"Oh, no, not at all! I moved out, remember?" Karen winked at Joseline. "I'm pretty happy where I am."

"She's only staying here a week though, right?" Joseline sat up straighter in her chair. "Then she's coming to stay with us for a week?"

"That's the plan." Merideth grinned at her sister, nodding agreeably. "That way none of us are hogging her."

"Sorry guys, do you mind if I interrupt?" Rider presented himself before the group, his hands clasped behind his back.

"That depends." Blake chortled, peeking behind him.

"Depends on what?" Rider asked, his features tense.

"On whether or not you're about to do something stupid," Blake quipped, taking a swig of his beer.

"Umm. No, I just needed to talk to Meri, and I kind of like all of you being here. Like witnesses," the other man stammered. Pulling the table away from the trio's feet, he cleared some room, then stepped over and sat on it so that he faced her. He brought his hands around to his lap, a bit of white box exposed.

"Don't do this, man," Blake warned. "I'm telling you. Go back in your room and wait for it."

"I'm tired of waiting," Rider sputtered, opening the lid. "We spent over a month in Virginia, and all I could think about was getting back here." Holding out the box, he showed

Meri his offering. "I tried to do this once before, but I made a mess of it. I hope this time you understand. You mean the world to me, Merideth Monroe. I would be so deeply honored if you would be my wife."

"What?" Karen asked, catching a fit of giggles next to his intended.

"He's asking me to marry him," Meri stated flatly. Her breathing shallow, she controlled her rage. "Rider? What did I tell you last time we talked about this?"

"That you wanted to wait until things were more settled." He glanced at the faces around them. "And they are. We're here in Boston. We have a great coven. We'll be ready to look for a house of our own soon. I think the timing is great to start planning our wedding."

"I don't want a wedding," Merideth clipped, standing her ground.

His face twisting into a grimace, Rider looked down at the beautiful ring he had chosen for her. "You want to elope?"

"Nope. I want you to put that ring back wherever you had it hidden, and never bring this up again."

"Wow," Sarah breathed next to her. "This is awkward."

"Sure is," Rider agreed, bobbing his head. "I thought you'd say yes." He closed the box. "You've turned me down twice now, Meri. I'm not sure I can recover from that. I mean, where do we go from here? Do we go back to just friend sex and pretend I never asked?" He gaped at her, not sure he would survive this time. "Is that what you really want?"

"It's always been friend sex, Rider. I told you when I moved in with you that I had plans. And they don't include marriage, or kids, or any of that mess." She glared at him, and no one else said a word.

Turning the box a few times, Rider studied the dimensions of it. Then he stood, placing it on the table where he'd been sitting. "You keep this, then. You hide it where you can find it, and maybe someday you'll feel like wearing it for me."

Stepping back over the table, he paused his retreat. "I'm going to go back to our room now. Actually, I'm going to move in with my clothes, if that's ok." He looked at Blake.

"Fine by me." The other man shrugged, the shit show before him beyond belief.

"Good. I'll be around to collect some of that friend sex some time," Rider dropped as he left the room and headed down the hall.

"What the hell was that?" Sarah gasped.

"That was some funny shit, right there." Karen cackled, holding her gut.

"Come on, guys, it wasn't that funny," Joseline pointed out, watching her sister's flushed face.

Feeling the tension in the moment, Blake turned to Sarah, fighting to hold a straight face. "How about you? You wanna get hitched?"

"What is it with you men and these lame ass proposals?" Meri asked indignantly. Throwing her arms across her chest, she leaned back against the cushions and glared at him.

Amused, Sarah giggled. "I never dreamed we were headed there." She batted her lashes at him and grinned.

"I bet I could scrounge up a ring." Blake gave his girl a tantalizing smile, indicating the box still sitting on the table.

"Hmm," Sarah mused. Her gaze locked with his, she waited, her breathing growing hard to detect. "I do like jewelry."

"Doesn't Sarah Korrigan have a nice melody?" he enticed. "And that would make you Mrs. Magister."

Sarah laughed at him. "You're so goofy. It's not like we're kismet or anything." She glanced over at Joseline, who also laughed.

"Oh, you two are just being silly," Karen goaded. "Kismet is my word."

"I don't know," Joseline teased. "They are pretty tight."

Sarah lay her hand across her pooched tummy. The doctor listened to the baby's heartbeat at her last visit, and she could hear it now thumping in her ears. "I think I want a Halloween wedding," she suggested.

"Isn't that your birthday?" Josee chided, scrunching her nose.

"Yeah, and it's only like six weeks away. How do you plan a wedding in that length of time?" Karen whined, afraid they were serious.

"Your belly is going to be huge," Merideth pointed out.

"It won't be that big," Sarah sniped, finally turning to face her. "I'm barely showing now as it is."

Blake ran his fingers around his lips, toying with them as he studied the girls, certain he had just gotten engaged. "I would love a Hallows Eve wedding."

Sarah returned her gaze to him. "Let's do it, Baby." She stood, scooching over to slide into his lap. Wrapping her arms around his shoulders, she kissed him. "Make me your bride, oh great one."

Blake coughed a laugh, then caught her neck with a firm hand. Pulling her down, he nuzzled her intimately. "You've made me so happy, Sarah. I couldn't imagine my life without you. Please tell me you're serious about this."

"Oh, I'm very serious. So serious, I'm already planning the dress," she agreed, using a hand to hold up the imaginary lace.

Unable to watch any longer, Merideth stood; snatching up the box, she retreated to her room. There, she found Rider, who had been gathering his things. "Where are you going?" she demanded, glaring at the painting of her he had leaned against the bathroom door to take with him.

"Are you kidding?" He glared at her. "I told you, I'm moving into the other apartment." He looked away, his face flushed. "I meant what I said about keeping the ring. And I wouldn't mind a little of that friend-sex later tonight if you're willing."

She shook her head. "I guess you think I'll change my mind now that Blake and Sarah are engaged."

Rider's features twisted in confusion. "They are? When did this happen?"

"Just now, after you stormed out," she mocked.

"Huh. I wonder if I'll be his best man," Rider pondered aloud, returning to his packing.

Meri stood with a stoic expression, watching until his chore was complete and he had disappeared into the bathroom, closing the door behind him. She waited until she heard the click of the latch before she allowed her tears to fall.

# Epilogue

"THIS PLACE IS GREAT," Rider observed. Running his hand along the top railing of the entryway to their new coffee nook, he grinned. "This contractor of yours does very nice work."

"Yeah, that would be why I hired him." Blake smirked at him. "I'm going to have Meri decorate it."

"Ah. She does nice work, too." Rider's shoulders drooped at the mention of his ex-girlfriend.

"Yup. She did the breakroom," Blake informed him, a little less smugly. Making his way around to the stairs, he called, "You get some of that friend-sex last night?"

"No," their enforcer replied, following him. "Merideth isn't actually speaking to me."

"Well, no mystery there." Blake chuckled, unlocking the door to the new office. Opening drawers in the desk, he rummaged around, then pulled out a simple flip phone. "Fucking dead. Where's the charger?" He searched again, locating it. Plugging it in, he tapped it. "I need to let this charge. Want some coffee?"

"Sure, I'll take a cup." He raised his chin towards the device. "That your secret phone for all your side action?"

"Meaning...?" Blake cut him a glance, then turned to cross the hall. In the breakroom, he filled the coffee pot with water from their new system.

"You know. Pussy. The ones you don't want Sarah knowing about." Rider stood in the doorway watching him. "Why else would you need a secret phone?"

"Who says it's a secret?" Blake asked, avoiding looking at him as he scooped the grounds.

"Well, you didn't take it with you to Virginia. That tells me it's for a side piece, and you didn't have time for that, so you left it here."

"You're assuming a lot." Blake laughed. Opening the credenza doors, he selected mugs and sat them next to the pot before meeting the other man's gaze. "I don't have a side piece. I'm a one-woman man these days, and Sarah's it. Has been since we met a couple of years ago."

"When your brother cursed her," Rider provided, taking a seat in one of the chairs.

"Yeah," Blake agreed shortly. Leaning against the cabinet, he watched the coffee drip for a moment. "I nearly lost her then. It would have killed me if I had. I know this must be hard for you, this thing with Merideth."

Rider shook his head slowly. "I'll live," he lied flatly, not certain of that in the least. He lifted his chin to study his friend. "I heard you and Sarah are getting married."

"Yeah." Blake grinned. "On Halloween. Very fitting since that's the night I almost lost her."

"How'd you get her to say yes?" Rider's voice had grown hollow, the sadness creeping in.

"I asked her." Blake shrugged. "If she'd said no, I'd have been fine with that. It was a joke anyways."

"A joke? You weren't serious?" Rider eyed him warily. "Did she know that?"

"Well, that's the thing. It was up to her. She could have laughed and played along. She got to make the call, and I let her."

"But you don't actually want to get married."

"I want her to be happy. She wants this, and I'm going to say my vows, and be the best damned husband I can be. You on the other hand..." Blake chuckled, pointing at him. "You are an idiot. I told you to put that ring back in your room, but you had to give it to her. With witnesses." He laughed again, reaching for the pot and pouring the cups. Placing them on the table, he sat across from him. "I'm sorry. I'm sure it wasn't funny to you." He leaned back, propping up his feet.

"The rest of you had a good laugh, though." Rider sulked, slurping his hot brew.

"Well, we laugh at most of the things you do," Blake confessed. "You say and do some crazy shit."

Rider looked away, unsure of where he stood. "I'm not sure I still fit in here."

"Don't start that," Blake said firmly. Sitting up, he leaned on the table towards him. "Women are like wounded animals. You can't corner them or they bite the fuck out of you. Everything she says and does is about doing things on her terms. You need to respect that, or you don't stand a chance."

"I don't think it will ever happen." Rider shook his head slowly. "I'm not sure it ever could have. She's too independent."

"Whatever man. Just stop cornering her. I need to check that phone." Blake stood, effectively ending the therapy session by exiting the room.

Following him, Rider grunted, "So, if that's not for a little something on the side, why do you need a secret phone?"

"Remember that day I went to visit my brother at the

prison?" Blake asked, then faltered. "Well, no. You guys were still in New Orleans, so probably not."

"No, but we heard about it. That's the day Sarah found out she was expecting," Rider recalled.

"Yes, it was." Blake sighed. "I wasn't actually there to visit my brother." He held the button, getting the phone to boot.

"So, what were you there for? I thought he's the one who told you she was pregnant."

"He did. I had to see him or the trip wouldn't have worked." He looked up, grinning. "I was there to recruit a guard to spy on him for me."

"Oh, huh." Rider curled his tongue, considering the prospect. "Have you learned anything useful?"

"Naw. He's never texted me anything, so I think it's a dead end. But we were gone a month, I figure I might as well look." His smile disappeared. "Oh my God, Rider, we have a message." He glared at the device.

Moving so he could read over his shoulder, Rider gasped. "What the fuck do we do now?"

Blake snapped the top closed, clenching his fist. "First off, we don't tell the girls. Then we figure out how we're going to handle this. We don't want to tip our hands until we're ready." Opening the phone, he replied.

"You're going to meet with your spy?"

"Yeah. Tonight, at the bar we used before. That way I can pay him in case he has anything else to share later."

"Good idea," Rider praised, then his features brightened. "Since I'm the enforcer, does that mean I get to be in on whatever you do to Hubert?"

"We have to be careful with that. He's Joseline's brother. If he's visiting Morcant, we have to find out if she knows about it." Blake scowled. "Maybe getting that pendant off her didn't really fix our problem."

"What problem?" Rider demanded. "What does this have to do with Josee?"

"I've been worried since we found her that she was working for my brother." Blake clenched his jaw, then added, "This is our first hard evidence that she really might be."

## Thank you

Thank you for sharing in this magical adventure! Please be sure to leave a review and don't miss the next installment of the Unexpected Magic Series ∼ Sam

Books in this series include:
    The Binding (book 1)
    The Wicked Awakened (book 2)
    The Secret Sibling (book 3)
    The Whisperer (book 4)
    The Magister's Child (book 5)

Boxed Sets
    The Unexpected Magical Opening Duo (books 1 and 2)

## About the Author

Anyone who knows me could tell you, I am a friendly kind of person, never met a stranger and take up conversations anywhere at any time. I work hard, and my mind never seems to shut down, as I wake up often in the middle of the night with ideas pouring out and demanding to be dealt with. Of course that means much of my books were written in the middle of the night.

I grew up and still live in the great state of Texas where everything is bigger, where we have warm weather and a central location. I love my state, my town, and my family, which includes my four sons, my significant other, and many friends as well.

I have thoroughly enjoyed writing this story and hope that you will love reading it just as much. And of course, there will be many more adventures to come.

You can follow Samantha Jacobey at:
Website: www.SamJacobey.com
Facebook: https://www.facebook.com/SamJacobey
Twitter: https://twitter.com/SamJacobey

# Also by SAMANTHA JACOBEY

http://www.amazon.com/-/e/B00GEB5LX0

**A New Life Series** – an epic adventure, TORI FARRELL's life IS one wild story... escaped from a biker gang and running from drug lords... used by the FBI and hoping to protect her present from her past... IT'S DARK - IT'S BRUTAL, and it's WORTH EVERY MINUTE OF IT!! (Mature read, 18+ for graphic sexual content and violence, including rape)

**Irrevocable Series** – Armageddon through the eyes of an entitled seventeen-year-old, BAILEY DEWITT's life has become a broken mess... after her parents died unexpectedly, she didn't think it could get any worse. But when the arrogance of man catches up and puts the entire world into a dooms-day spiral, there will be only one place she can run to - the one place she wanted desperately to escape. Can she and Caleb build a life together when the world is falling apart? (New Adult)

**Teach Me to Prey** – in this standalone thriller, JASON TRUITT and his friends have gotten their way for years. Deceit, sex, and foul play aren't normally covered in the curriculum, but they're doing whatever it takes to get under BECKY STEWART's skin. When one of the boys turns up dead, it's a race against time to save the others; a STUNNING STORY that will get your heart racing and leave you breathless by the end... (New Adult)

**Sweet Christmas Series** - Life isn't always sweet, even for girls called Candy. Candice Parker's life has never been easy. Plagued by losses and setbacks, each day is a struggle for the petite brunette and her young son. When fireman Gary enters her world, he is one mistake she refuses to make; but after tragedy strikes, she may not have a choice. (New Adult)

# Also From The Lavish Family

**Fairfield Corners Series**

L.A. Remenicky

https://www.lavishpublishing.com/authors/l-a-remenicky/

Small town romance with a paranormal twist! Each in standalone style, read and enjoy any order, any number!

**Saving Cassie – Book 1**: Some secrets are too dangerous to keep.

After ten years in the big city, Cassie Holt is back in Fairfield Corners. She may look like the same girl who left home a decade before but she's hiding a dark truth from everyone. When her life is threatened by the demons of her past, her best friend—who happens to be the local sheriff—offers his help.

Deputy Logan Miller has been burned by love. He's not looking to get involved but duty calls when the sheriff tasks him with Cassie's protection. Thrown into close quarters with the gorgeous bookseller, sparks fly. Logan is drawn to Cassie, but it's hard to get close to someone who keeps themselves guarded all the time.

To keep Cassie safe, Logan must open his heart but that's something he swore he'd never do.

**Ragan's Song – Book 2**: One look into his eyes told her she was in trouble – again!

Ragan returned home to celebrate her parent's anniversary hoping they would forgive her the secrets she's kept from them over the last few years. When she discovered that Adam was still living in Fairfield Corners she hoped her secrets were safe, secrets that drove her away three years, secrets that could change both their lives forever.

Adam Bricklin was devastated when Ragan Newlin left town. No note, no email, no text. She was just gone. It has taken three years for Adam to finally move past the heartbreak he suffered when Ragan left town. Now he's moved on and everything was going well until the day Ragan returned to Fairfield Corners. Now the melody that he lost all those years ago is back. It's the same tune he heard that tells him right from wrong—the one that sang Ragan was the one.

Even separation can't silence Adam and Ragan's song, and now that she's back it's time for Adam to decide if he should let the song die or breathe life into it once again.

**Where There's Faith – Book 3**: A past she can't remember. A love he can't forget.

After losing everything in an accident that he can only blame himself for, Robbie Newlin embraced sobriety and tried to live his life quietly alone at this family's cottage on the lake. Grief being his only ally, Robbie was perfectly content with how he lived until Faith moved into the cottage next door. Now Faith had him questioning whether to keep grieving or to open his broken heart to let love in again.

Faith McMillan had no memory of her life before that day three years ago. The physical scars had faded but the emotional ones were still fresh and raw. Living rent-free seemed like a great way to finish her second book and give her the time to figure out her next move, but then she met the reclusive guy next door and everything changed.

To get past the broken parts, Robbie and Faith must figure out if they want to continue living their lives in solitude or take a chance on finding an ending together.

## Behind Blue Eyes Series

Sara J. Bernhardt

https://www.lavishpublishing.com/authors/sara-j-bernhardt/

A father's desire to save his child presents him with an unthinkable choice that leaves him darker than human, forced to roam through time alone as he searches for the place he belongs.

**Adam Gold – Book 1**: Fleeing the French invasion of Geneva Switzerland in the 1700s, Adam Gold books passage to America with his family. On the ship, Adam's daughter falls fatally ill. A mysterious man comes to Adam with a way to save his child by turning Adam into something darker than human.

**The Medallion – Book 2**: Adam Gold, an immortal with sweet eyes of blue, rushes through the centuries on a quest for reason and a thirst for revenge. To cope with his pain and regret, he sleeps away the years and awakes in a new era with a powerful, ancient vampire who sets her sights on him.

**Golden Shackles – Book 3**: When the ancient queen, Sekhmet snatches up Adam, he is faced with a terrifying decision. To help aid her in her vile plans or dare to stand against her.

Plus 3 more segments!

## **Between the Trees**

Kathy Moczerniak

https://www.lavishpublishing.com/authors/kathy-moczerniak/

A beautiful coming of age with a dark side that one teenager must fight to overcome...

Beyond Kathryn Lucas' first memory of her father's tree lay a dysfunctional path of violence, heartbreak, and secrets within a family severely entrenched in the vicious cycle of abuse. A lifetime of fear drives her from her home, and the teenage girl finds refuge with an aunt and uncle determined to protect their niece.

Distressing flashbacks unravel in Kathryn's fragile mind among the turmoil encircling her as she struggles through adolescence and descends into her pain-ridden past. When the summation of her unsettling memories allows the darkness to overtake her, she becomes desperate to unearth the light.

Inspired by a true story, Kathryn must hold on tightly to those who love her, searching for her place in a world threatening to break her as she fights to overcome life's betrayals before she is deprived of her future.